Literary editor of th
Terence de Vere W
novelist and cont

NAME IS
ORVAL

Terence de Vere White

Futura

A Futura Book

First published in Great Britain in 1978 by
Victor Gollancz Ltd, London

This edition published in 1986 by Futura Publications,
a Division of Macdonald & Co (Publishers) Ltd
London & Sydney

ISBN 0 7088 2942 2

Printed in Great Britain by
The Guernsey Press Co. Ltd
Guernsey, Channel Islands

Futura Publications
A Division of
Macdonald & Co (Publishers) Ltd
Maxwell House
74 Worship Street
London EC2A 2EN

A BPCC plc Company

For Russell Murphy

Part 1

I

MISS KELLY WAS very rich. Not that it did her much good, some people said. But they were wrong. To assess how essential her wealth was to her existence one had only to imagine Miss Kelly penniless. And penniless, Miss Kelly could hardly have existed. What those critics might have sustained, if it came to argument, was that marriage might have come her way had she put a lower value on herself. She was quite good looking still, and must have been handsome when she was young. But she combined stupidity with conceit; and with the passage of time, this gave her face the expression of a swan at bay. Her parents died when she was a child, and she grew up with a much older half-brother, who was even more stupid and infinitely more conceited than herself. To him she was devoted, and his word was law. He had the Kelly pedigree, reading back to the original tribal chieftain, framed in the hall of their substantial house. Pope Pius XII had conferred an order upon him for his signal services to the church. He was a Knight of Malta, and looked splendid in the insignia of that historic fraternity. Michael Kelly, acting *in loco parentis*, put his sister's admirers to rout. Some because he spied them as fortune-hunters, others because they were inferior to her in social pretensions; and a select few, lacking in no other respect, were turned away because they were not of the Church of Rome.

The Duke of Norfolk, had he presented himself, would have had all the necessary qualifications; but he failed to appear; a French nobleman advanced too rapidly and frightened Miss Kelly away; there was an American, but he was kept on a string and got bored. He was not the only one; Miss Kelly's emotions never approached fever heat; even after her brother died (unmarried) leaving her to face the world with three-quarters of a million pounds, she adopted Fabian tactics whenever a suitor appeared. Before she had made up her mind, he had decided, inevitably, that life with Miss Kelly would be dull.

She entertained; she travelled; she kept a horse in training; she knew three sociable queers all prepared, at short notice, to fill an empty place at dinner or accompany her where a woman needs an escort. Her body had the aura of a parcel from a fashionable store that has not yet been unpacked; but she had a healthy appetite; she was quite substantial; there was nothing about her (except her clothes) that was not essentially common-place and down to earth. She would have liked to have been married, and at fifty-two had not ruled out the possibility. Her mind, not given to fantasy as a rule, unfed by fiction—she read hardly at all—entertained a romantic day-dream. A handsome man of suitable age (in circumstances which she had not worked out in detail) would appeal to her for assistance, which she (recognising good breeding at a glance) would give him unques-tioning. Later he would return and disclose himself—a Steward of the Jockey Club, a Swiss General, a Spanish Count. . . . He would propose marriage, and during the decent interval when she was supplying herself with the necessaries for that con-dition, would—if not already of the right persuasion—undergo instruction from a sympathetic Jesuit. This last was a condition imposed in loyalty to Michael who died before Vatican II and maintained a rigidity on all points of discipline that it was now almost impossible to expect. Respect for her beliefs—chief of which was detestation of socialism in any guise—was all she would insist upon if a dignified bearing, good manners and freedom from vice were guaranteed. As these conditions were written in to any horse purchase, it was not unreasonable to expect them with a husband.

Not to anybody would Miss Kelly have disclosed her silly dream. She knew it was silly; but she couldn't always be the dignified, prudent, reserved lady that Michael had approved. She had a frolicsome side when she threw back her head and laughed. Not at jokes, as a rule; she didn't see jokes, and discouraged conversations that were not predictable. Her ideal man would be distinguished without being clever, devoted without being amorous; not so poor to have to depend for his keep on her nor yet rich enough to be indifferent to the substan-tial benefits of a connection with the invested profits of three generations engrossed in the manufacture of artificial manure.

This fancy was playful; nothing went very deep with Miss Kelly. Her complaints were chiefly about the hardships of the times, the deterioration of standards, the almost total absence of service, even when one was prepared to pay for it.

A slight but persistent cough for which her doctor gave her a prescription and advised a change of air explained her appearance alone in a guest house in County Donegal. Situated close to the sea with the great peaks of Mount Errigal to the north and Derrick Hill to the south-east, Carrow House was more suitable to her desire for exclusiveness than a hotel. It was shamelessly expensive and patronised mostly by foreigners. Miss Kelly had not intended to come by herself; she could usually count on Aggie Fitzsimons as a companion anywhere she went, but Aggie had tiresomely some family call to answer, and Cyril Forbes was maddeningly engaged for dinners from which he refused to excuse himself, but promised to come at the end of the next week and explore the caves at Derrick Hill; he even suggested an attempt to scale Mount Errigal. Cyril was highly amusing. No wonder he was in such constant demand by hostesses. In the meanwhile, Miss Kelly breakfasted in bed, read the newspaper slowly, and spent a good deal of each day on the telephone. She had several friends with pleasant homes in the county; it was quite a business arranging to see them and planning a pay-back dinner of her own after Cyril arrived when he could pair off with her.

As she had not announced her arrival in advance, invitations tended to crowd the last days of her stay. The time before Cyril arrived was interrupted only by a lunch with an American widow who was an authority on the life of St Patrick, but stingy where food was concerned. Otherwise, Miss Kelly had to depend upon her own resources unless she made friends with some of the residents. They were mostly French or German, had come for fishing, left noisily after breakfast, and returned noisily in time for dinner. They were self-contained; and except to

11

bid her the time of day, were not going to include Miss Kelly in their plans. A pair of earnest friendly American spinsters of about her own age represented everything Miss Kelly repudiated at sight. She crushed them twice a day with a formal bow. There were couples with children, who exchanged a few words in the hall, going and coming, two priests who enjoyed the food, and a sad pair with a mongol child.

There was television; but Miss Kelly felt she was cheapening herself when she watched it in a public room. A book had its advantages in this respect; it explained a demand for privacy. But Miss Kelly could never concentrate for ten minutes together on a book for the good reason that she never came to terms with her own inclinations. There were writers who made large fortunes by catering for Miss Kelly's tastes, who shared her repugnance to all that is not nice in life and kept romance free from undermining detail. Instead of reading these—on the same principle that she avoided people of no consequence—she encumbered herself with whatever she saw praised in *The Times* and sent herself to sleep reading statesmen's memoirs and the eventless lives of authors she had never read. She rarely finished a book, and after three *Lives* of Queen Victoria still did not know when she died. Matters which were boring and impossible to follow in conversation were not cured of either defect—rather the offence was compounded—when they were dealt with at length in books. Consequently, Miss Kelly's eyes spent little time on the printed page; but she noticed in detail what everyone round her was wearing and she took in the house's furnishings. She was used to good things, and if she did not always recognise them in unlikely surroundings, she had an unfailing nose for detecting fakes.

From living alone she had acquired the habit of bolting her food, and the plates before her were changed with a rapidity that promised her departure from the dining-room before the other residents had finished their main course. She brought the apple tart to anchor before her and lit a cigarette. Smoking gave her no pleasure—nothing gave her very much—but she liked the picture of herself smoking—she liked to assume poses that she thought fitted her—nobody could handle a telephone receiver with more grace. She would occupy herself looking sibylline and taking stock, through the smoke, of her fellow guests until they had caught up with her. To say that she was looking for attention, "going on for notice", would expose an inability to understand Miss Kelly's approach to life. Hers was the attitude of a public figure who takes for granted her interest to the spectators and is only concerned to be suitably accoutred for the particular occasion. Handsomely dressed on all occasions, well-mounted on horseback, in the best seats at every entertainment, it never occurred to her that there could be any doubt about her significance. The dignity of Michael's manner, in private as in public, had been a model; from her half-brother and mentor Miss Kelly acquired a sense of her own importance, which required no buttress and was proof against any assault.

There was nobody in the room that she would have cared to strike up an acquaintance with, she decided. A man of a certain age, in a party consisting of two French couples, interested her somewhat, because he had a way of saying very little, and that in a deep voice which reminded her of a character in an old film. She wondered if the same performance in English would be so effective; not that she would ever have preferred any foreigner, however deep his bass, to an Englishman of the right type. They were getting scarce; there was none in this room. As if she had commanded a genie the dining-room door opened at that instant, admitting a single man.

The late-comer was about Miss Kelly's age or a few years older. Tall, quietly dressed, lean—there was something in his diffident manner which appealed to her after the good-humoured din of the foreign bodies—and she welcomed his presence as an ally. There were details in men's appearance her brother had taught her to look for before she vouchsafed approval: tailoring, shoes, hair-cut, position of handkerchief —external and visible signs of inward grace. The newcomer was at least someone whom Michael would not have frozen into silence if he attempted to address him. He would have been allowed his say. His arrival gave interest to the meal, Miss Kelly

13

further postponed engagement with the apple tart and lit another cigarette.

The man in the corner—as she christened him—looked at the menu and gave an order to the waiter at his elbow. His face was well-modelled with high cheek-bones; the mouth more canine than Miss Kelly cared for (it belied the reassuring streaks of grey in his side hair). In his pale eyes there was a detached, almost glazed expression. He seemed quite indifferent to the presence of other guests, didn't glance at them, was taken up apparently with his own thoughts. Then he looked up, and Miss Kelly met his full gaze. At first it was neutral: he might have been thinking about something else and not have seen her—the manner in which he checked his wandering survey and came back, as it were, to look again, suggested this. Whatever caused him to take a second look, the result was dramatic. His face crumpled, went white; he couldn't take his frightened eyes off her. On only one point was Miss Kelly unshakeable; she had never seen his face before. Never. It was utterly new, unprecedented and—were she not in a crowded dining-room—alarming. She had never been the victim of any assault or robbery, never suffered any harm or ill that was criminal in its character; if she had, she would not have doubted that she was now confronting the malefactor. With a visible effort, the stranger looked down at his plate; Miss Kelly took up the book about Teilhard de Chardin she had carried round with her for the last few weeks, and the drama was over; but every now and then she took a peep into the corner, and sometimes she caught him looking at her with the same haunted expression.

His manner was now composed, and his face had lost its pallor, was flushed somewhat. She was intrigued and ordered brandy with coffee to prolong the meal. She no longer pretended to read; her mind was more richly entertained than it had been for weeks. Now she was grateful to Cyril for not having come at once to her call. Had he been here she would have missed this extraordinary experience. Her explanation of it was that she had been mistaken for someone else, and now realising his mistake, the unfortunate man was embarrassed. Did she resemble a divorced wife or—more exciting—a discarded mistress?

14

Neither, however ill-met, could have aroused that expression; it was not mere surprise, closer to horror, as if he had seen a ghost. That was it. She looked like someone he knew who was dead. It sometimes happened. Miss Kelly was not imaginative; the idea did not arouse any necrophilic fantasy. Indeed, her reaction was not unmixed with amusement. She was intrigued, more intrigued than she had been for many years, had ever been, perhaps, because she had no formula for dealing with this situation as she had, for instance, in the restraining of male advances: a Plimsoll mark below which she was theoretically in danger. She must prepare herself so that if they got into conversation she could turn the misunderstanding to advantage without treading on corns. "Gosh," she said to herself, recalling his expression, "he did look upset.". Tom Stafford hadn't looked as ghastly as that when his horse fell on the flat, cantering home alone in the Derby. He had gone green and come out in a lather of sweat, but didn't have that chamber-of-horrors look. That was something she had never seen before, and she was the last person—she would, with reason, have said—to inspire it. She observed that the stranger had refused a pudding, and taken no brandy with his coffee or lit a cigarette. He might leave at any moment. She swallowed her drink and then, with a queenly smile to the waiter, walked out of the room, looking neither to right nor left, grateful now that she had put on the dress which a few hours ago had seemed too good for the occasion.

The establishment endeavoured to preserve the atmosphere of a country house; there was no general lounge as in a hotel; the usual suite of living-rooms were available for guests. Miss Kelly was immediately faced with a problem, where to seat herself. If she took up her position on a sofa in the hall it was possible that the fascinating diner would simply lack the courage to come and talk to her; but he might miss her if she stationed herself in one of the other rooms. He did not look like a man who would watch television in company, more like the sort of man who would . . . Miss Kelly saw what she must do with an unusual gleam of inspiration; it was a summer night; there were benches at each side of the hall door commanding a noble prospect; sitting there

15

she would be seen by anyone in the hall, so that the man, if he looked around, could not miss her, and if he joined her on the terrace, they would fall into conversation naturally.

No time to fetch a wrap—fortunately the night was warm, although there were autumnal signs in the air—Miss Kelly went out on the steps. Later, others might come; but just now they were debouching from the dining-room and settling down indoors.

Suppressing a childlike urge to look over her shoulder—it would spoil the whole effect if she were caught—she lit yet another cigarette. One after meals was her usual ration. The cigarette refused to burn; she took out her lighter; it wouldn't work.

"Can I . . .?"

"Oh, thank you."

There is no social gesture more gracefully intimate than this. Miss Kelly took three strong puffs to keep the fire burning.

"I see you are admiring the view," she said. "Is this your first visit to Donegal?"

"I was never here before."

His accent was reassuring; Irish or English? She couldn't be certain. But there was a note of strain in the voice; glancing at him through smoke she saw that he looked agitated.

Her conversational techniques provided no alternatives. For her there was only one road to acquaintance: it was paved with platitudes. She chose the first that came to mind.

"I'm afraid we are seeing the end of summer."

He let the observation die in silence, then he said, "You must forgive me for staring at you like that in the dining-room; but you looked so like someone else, you quite startled me."

"Why should the resemblance frighten you?"

"Because the person I thought you were is dead."

"Oh, how unpleasant—sad, I mean."

"A long time ago. You're taller. I noticed that when you were leaving the dining-room."

"You have been staring at me, I must say. I don't know that I altogether liked it."

"I'm sorry if I have offended you."

16

"Oh, I am not offended. It is only that one isn't used to being—what's the word?—put under a microscope."

"You're Miss Kelly, aren't you?"

"Yes. I don't think I ever met you before."

"I saw your name in the register. You haven't relations, by any chance, called Truell?"

"No. I don't think so."

"Or Adams? or Forsythe?"

"I am sure not. I haven't looked at our pedigree—it's at home—for ages, but those names don't ring a bell. My mother's name was Blake. We have Joyces, O'Flahertys and other West of Ireland names on her side. Ryan, Kennedy, Despard, Synnot on my father's."

The man made a gesture of impatience.

"I didn't mean to be inquisitive. The person you reminded me of was a Truell, and I just mentioned other close relations. I never saw such an absolute likeness. Your voice is not the same; but it is much easier to recollect the face than the voice of someone who is long dead. What a shock one would get if one heard the voice again; and yet, sometimes—not very often—I hear quite distinctly a voice calling out my name."

"How very peculiar. You mean this person, this dead person, you mistook me for."

He didn't answer. He was restless, as if uncertain whether to move or stay. He would have to offer to sit beside her, she decided. She wouldn't make the suggestion. Then she had yet another inspiration.

"Would you be so kind as to see whether you can make my lighter work? I don't know what's up with it. I filled it only a few days ago, and I use it hardly at all. Would you like one of my cigarettes, by the way? I should have offered you one for coming so nobly to my rescue."

"I'm not very lucky myself with lighters," he said. But he took Miss Kelly's and, as she hoped, sat down beside her.

He had this way of not answering questions, waving them aside or, perhaps not hearing them. Miss Kelly noticed how his hands were trembling as he fiddled with the lighter.

"Splendid," she said, when a flame leaped up. "You *are* clever."

Again he made a gesture indicating impatience with the wall of inanity she was erecting between them.

"I always say—" she began.

He interrupted. "I was so certain it was this other person that I was coming over to speak to you. Then I remembered she was dead. You must have thought my behaviour extraordinary. Even now I can't get over the likeness." He looked into Miss Kelly's eyes. His own were feverish. She didn't particularly like that.

Moving very slightly on the bench, in a voice that was too obviously conciliatory, she asked him who this person was. It did not seem, in the circumstances—and he had introduced the theatrical note—unreasonable to enquire. If it was someone—as she sensed—that he loved, there were euphemisms in plenty to convey that, and she, of course, would respect his reticence. A nod was as good as a wink, her mother used to say. What would her mother have said if she were listening to this extraordinary conversation? When she thought about her mother, Miss Kelly forgot she was fifty-two.

The question increased his agitation. He looked round him and then, his eyes full of trouble, said: "Are you staying here for long?"

"A fortnight."

"We might go for a walk tomorrow. Are you alone?"

"I am."

"I came for a few days. The place was recommended to me. I don't care for large hotels."

"You live in England?"

"No, I've been abroad for a great many years."

"I like travel," Miss Kelly said. "Next year I've planned to go down the Nile with friends of mine."

"I'm going in," he said.

He has no manners, Miss Kelly decided.

"So shall I. It's beginning to turn cold, and I came to Donegal to get over a boring cough I couldn't shake off."

"It wasn't very sensible, then, to sit out of doors without even a wrap."

"You know how it is. I caught sight of the view as I came out of the dining-room and I just plopped myself down to enjoy it. I can't understand people who come to a place like this with such fabulous scenery and spend their time indoors."

"They've been out all day, I suppose."

He cut off completely, Miss Kelly couldn't fail to notice, as if he had suddenly lost interest. His eyes, she remembered, had an unseeing, an inward look before he had seen her in the dining-room. A very private person, she would have said, who lived alone and took little or no interest in other people. He had returned to that character now.

"I hope you enjoy your stay," she said in the porch. They were back, among people.

He looked ill at ease and made no suggestion that she should sit with him here. She had had no intention of retiring at this time of evening, but now it seemed the easiest line of retreat.

"I must nurse my cold," she explained.

He nodded, uninterested.

"And thank you for fixing my lighter."

No response. He was the oddest man she had ever met.

Early to bed, she would be down early and look up his name in the register. He should have supplied it unasked. It was, in the circumstances, when he knew hers, rather remiss of him, but, then, he didn't seem to want to give away any information about himself. He avoided her questions, and his "abroad" might be anywhere. All she knew was that he had two more days to put in, and he had suggested a walk. He could hardly back out of that unless he was very odd indeed. She had a pair of slacks that fitted like a dream and a white turtle-neck jumper of angora wool. A becoming outfit; it only remained for the weather to hold up and tomorrow might be interesting. She had plenty to think about in bed, and no occasion to have recourse to Teilhard de Chardin. The stranger had glanced at the title, she noticed. That was what the book was for.

She was up early and, while engaged in conversation in the hall with the proprietor's wife, glanced at the visitors' book. Since her own arrival there had been but one other: H. Robinson, with an address in Perth, Western Australia.

19

The entry gave her food for all the thought she was capable of at breakfast. As a name, it did not fit her ideal man; but did not necessarily preclude the possibility of distinction, if only vast wealth, as to which, whether one needed it or not, there was always something reassuring about the sound. And it was unfair to dismiss the possibility of his being someone well-bred—there must be some by this time in Australia, although she had never heard of one. When Mr Robinson saw that her name was Kelly, he, too, may have had reservations; but he had persisted, and whatever there may have been about last evening's encounter, he cannot but have carried away from it the portrait of a lady. A well-brought-up girl Miss Kelly had been, as her mother before her; and as such she remained. She soon got over the sensation of having been let down, and had to confess to herself that she had played absurdly and romantically with the possibility of a title, high army rank, even a judgeship. She had come to an age when an admirer of whom she could be proud should have attained his professional ambition. "Judge Robinson" would have satisfied her. There was something respectworthy about it. H. Robinson might own a chain of grocery stores; but, if he did, better he should do so in Perth, Western Australia. She couldn't see herself emigrating to such an outlandish place. If Mr Robinson and she were to unite their lives it would be on her ground, in her house, among her friends and acquaintances. She had never considered any other possibility. Except that she had grown older and servants had become increasingly difficult to find, life, in essentials, hadn't changed for Miss Kelly. The world around her had, at a pace that sometimes alarmed her. She found herself talking about things and using words that would have brought on apoplexy were Michael alive to hear her; but it didn't really mean anything. In theory she knew a great deal that her brother would have been offended by if she mentioned it, but she remained innocent to the extent that she could not imagine herself putting any of this knowledge to use.

Brooding over last evening, Mr Robinson's dramatic appearance and behaviour—like something in a magazine story—she recognised a pattern that all her encounters with the opposite sex had taken since she left school. She could only be herself; her mind worked on a simple practical basis; allowing for the temporary influence of changes in health or temperature, she always felt the same. She used to like it if a young man, of a sort she approved, paid her attention; she was quite jealous when she saw another girl preferred; but, somehow, conversation always seemed to take the same course, and if her companion grasped her hand or showed signs of becoming familiar she never knew what to do. It was like being given an electric toy without a plug to attach it to the mains. She said something invariably that made the situation ludicrous. The experiment was never repeated. She had been mauled in her time by men in a disagreeable condition of intoxication; but she was strong enough to keep a marauder of that predictable kind within controllable limits. There were men who were notorious pouncers or desperately bored. Sometimes they apologised next day, which was always nice, and restored one's faith in humanity. She understood the wisdom of not getting into these situations, and had learned to practise it successfully. When she went out, it was usually in her own expensive car, and when she had an escort, he was a passenger. Men came to stay in her house, but she never stayed under the roof of a single man. And none had ever asked her to. There were words that she did not have to look up in the dictionary; but they conveyed only as much meaning as the geometry she had learned at school. The three angles of a triangle are together equal to two right angles. She had been taught that, and did not dispute its essential truth; but if anyone had invited her to demonstrate the proposition she would have been completely at a loss. Her knowledge of sex was on the same plane, and, perhaps, better illustrated by the science of algebra, in which the nuns had also instructed her. There was this mysterious factor x: x could be made equal to anything. She was content to live on the basis that if she found herself in an unfamiliar situation—the x-factor would be introduced, and would supply what had been missing from the proposition when she assented to it. Except on the level of gossip, she was practically without curiosity, and content that one day should be very much like another, on condition that she ordained the over-all pattern.

21

Mr Robinson, if he were to marry her, would take the empty place in her house previously occupied by her brother—except in the matter of bedroom occupancy and, of course, though it need not be mentioned, the x-factor nature supplied in these circumstances. His life would be transformed, hers added to only in one particular.

Miss Kelly had no doubt that the change which took place in Mr Robinson's manner during their short conversation on the terrace was of a piece with her lifelong experience of men when they tried to improve their acquaintance with her. He thought she was standoffish. If he repeated that invitation to come for a walk, she would make it her business to let him know that she was not remote or unattainable. He would find, if he were patient, that she was as romantic as a schoolgirl and—lonely in the modern world—had kept her dream intact. The man who won her would experience the thrill of the discoverer of the North West Passage.

Her thoughts were racing now: she had to pull herself up with an almost physical effort. Mr Robinson had been upset by her likeness to someone he had known, someone, obviously, who had meant a great deal to him. Having discovered his mistake, he might well be irritated by his unguarded behaviour. His rapid change of mood could have been due to a depressing realisation that the resemblance was only skin deep. Truell had been the name of this double. She would like to discover her first name. It could be a bond. If she were called Margaret, for instance. Margaret was Miss Kelly's sainted mother's name. If she could she would find this out, it might strike a sympathetic chord. Next time she must avoid whatever it was had disappointed him in her. She tried to recall the conversation from the moment he offered so gallantly to light her cigarette. She had no experience of any feeling that persisted or went deeper than was comfortable to bear or that a course of mild distraction could not cure. She didn't object to Mr Robinson's being serious. A humorist in the house would be intolerable. She just didn't want a funereal atmosphere. But she could hardly contemplate the possibility of such an extreme.

When, as she was eating the very last piece of toast, Mr

Robinson, dressed for the country, appeared in the dining-room, she had so well recruited her usual good spirits that she greeted him with a smile guaranteed to sweep away any vestige of unease that might have lingered with him overnight. He nodded civilly, and then fell to breakfasting behind a newspaper. When she realised that the barrier would not come down, she went out; she did not look in his direction, but, when she passed, he put down his paper and took a long look that would have astonished her.

Where to place herself? To be found on the same seat on the terrace alone would not do. She selected a chair that could be seen by anyone coming out of the dining-room, and pretended to read an out-of-date newspaper which happened to be lying on the hall table. Mr Robinson did not hurry over his breakfast; she sensed rather than saw him come into the hall, pause, and then, when she had put down the *Donegal Democrat* and looked up, come across the hall. The haunted expression had left his face, but there was still about it an air of preoccupation.

"Good morning," Miss Kelly said, "I hope you slept well."

"I never sleep well in a strange bed," Mr Robinson replied.

His eye then travelled to Miss Kelly's newspaper, and she hoped he was not gifted with long sight.

"Some people are like that. My half-brother—my late half-brother I should say—used to motor back miles after a party rather than stay the night."

Mr Robinson narrowed his eyes slightly, but added nothing in words.

"Did you say you had stayed here before?" she enquired, to break the silence.

"I did not."

Discouraged but persevering, she remarked that it was her own first time, but that she hadn't settled in yet.

"There is fishing," she said, "if you fish, and I'm told the golf at Rosapenna is first class: I don't play golf myself. I promised the friends who sent me here that I would go and look at the cliffs at Slieve League. They were ecstatic about the view. I thought I might drive there this afternoon if the weather holds up."

"Are you going with someone?"

"No. Would you like to come? It's not much more than an hour's drive. We would be back in good time for dinner."

Mr Robinson seemed to consider; then he said he would like to. He hadn't a car of his own and had thought about hiring one.

"You are welcome to the loan of mine," she was about to say, and then thought better of it.

"I'll look forward to that," Mr Robinson said.

"You will be lunching here?"

"Yes."

"I'll see you then."

Nervousness had made her say something calculated to drive him away. If only he would sit down and talk about the weather instead of hovering. It made her nervous. Although he looked quite calm, she sensed tension. If she knew him better she might hope to soothe him down. He reminded her of a horse she once had—all nerves, afraid of nothing—but she rode it in terror, never knowing what devil might get into it, and exchanged it before the season was out for a large comfortable gelding. She could manage that.

"I've letters to write," Mr Robinson said.

"I'm glad you said that. You've reminded me of one that's on my conscience," Miss Kelly said.

"Don't let me hold you up."

He gave her then a most curious look; "from under his eyes", was how she described it. She had become accustomed to his stare; that had been accounted for; he was tracing a likeness; this was something else; concentrated and detached at the same time, as if he were making a calculation. It was uncanny. Then he stalked away.

Miss Kelly, never having known any man intimately, except her brother (and he was the most remote of mortals), allowed men a very wide latitude in their behaviour. Setting great store on formal manners, punctuality, and matters of etiquette, because they affected her, she would excuse under a prescription capsulated into "Oh, *men*", a wide range of practices. In this she was a relic of Victorianism when women in her position were protected from life, and knew only vaguely about

24

brutalities in the world of their men. To her it was all-important—especially since she discovered he came from Australia and had such an unpromising name—that Mr Robinson had the appearance of the men she encountered in her world, who—some of them—wondered if marriage to her would be worth the material advantages it would bring, and, up to the present, had decided it would not.

Therefore, that cold stare did not upset her as much as a lapse into an Australian accent would certainly have. Michael, who was a model, had been as cold as ice.

The morning that had looked so long when she woke up, was not long enough to allow her to fit in all the things she suddenly wanted to do, including a search in the guide book for references to Slieve League so that she would have something intelligent ready to say when they arrived there. Men were made irritable by inefficient driving: she studied the road map carefully. Her friends had advised that the climb to the summit was rather tricky; the thing to do was to drive to Bunglass where there was a plateau from which one had an uninterrupted view of the cliffs, rising, the guide book told her, 2,000 feet from the Atlantic.

There was not—she was grateful—too much to take in. She would remember to tell him that "the summit itself affords one of the most remarkable panoramas in Europe", and if he chose to argue about it, she could produce the book to support her claim. Michael had contradicted everything she said, so that there was no fear of a rupture with Mr Robinson if he adopted the same tactics. Those were not the sort of things that made her fall out with people. If there were time after they had looked at the view—and that couldn't take long—they might go on to Glencolumkille where, she had heard, tea with home-made scones was served.

At lunchtime, from her window, she saw him coming back from a walk along the local cliffs, unspectacular in comparison with what they would see this afternoon; but it gave her an opportunity to study him unobserved. Michael was still her model of manly looks. He had carried himself bolt upright, to such an extent that he had an appearance of being permanently offended. Mr Robinson had a straight back and long legs, but there was the grace of an animal in his movements; he didn't—like Michael—seem to be on perpetual sentry-go. As he passed under her window he looked up unexpectedly. She blushed, but if he saw her he gave no sign. He had still all his hair, she noticed.

She was fascinated, more than she had ever been perhaps, because she was on unfamiliar territory, and it was the first time in her life that she had ever struck up an acquaintance on her own, away from friends. It might be a disaster, and she would long then for Cyril to come, who would be gossipy and cosy and restfully predictable. It would almost certainly end in vague politeness and a card at Christmas; but that wouldn't break her heart. It never had. Meanwhile, she could indulge her harmless fantasy and let Aggie Fitzsimons have an account of it that would mildly raise her hair. Nothing ever happened to dear Aggie. Miss Kelly went down late to lunch, and noticed with disappointment signs of a finished meal on Mr Robinson's table. He was a tantalising man. She ate her own lunch slowly, exercising admirable control. It was now two o'clock. He was standing about in the hall when she came out, and she suggested an immediate departure after she had collected a raincoat in her room.

"I'll wait for you here," he said.

His manner was listless. Was he regretting the arrangement? She would not suggest tea afterwards unless he brought up the subject. There was a small cloud over her morning spirits; but, she told herself, putting some scent behind her ears, it might be as well that she didn't start out in what she saw now was a romantic mood.

II

MISS KELLY PRIDED herself on her ability to drive a car. It was one of the arts that she had mastered, and as she had an expensive machine, kept in perfect condition, she was possibly more confident behind a driving wheel than in any other position. Mr Robinson made no effort to talk or even to look about him; and Miss Kelly gave up exclaiming at the views along the road when her enthusiasm met no response. After leaving Carrick she concentrated very hard so as not to mistake the road. A sign pointing to Bunglass told her that her mission was accomplished; the road from this point became a spiral staircase; up and up, round and round, ending abruptly on a large platform provided by nature, it seemed, as a place to view from. Across the bay a vast cliff rose from the sea. There were three motor cars parked on Bunglass, and their occupants were scattered round the hilltop.

Miss Kelly parked her car carefully; she would have liked Mr Robinson to leap out and open her door for her, but he remained in his place until she suggested that they get out and look at the view. The hill on which they stood did not have a sheer drop; there were grassy hollows round about, and in one of these Miss Kelly spread the car rug. "We get a perfect view from here," she said, taking out her guide book. Before sitting down, she peeped cautiously over the knoll behind which she had laid her rug and gave a little cry of alarm to discover how close she was to the edge. She did not have a good head for heights and seagulls circling against the great wall across the narrow stretch of water looked so far down that, for a moment, she felt dizzy. It was a golden afternoon; the only sound was a faint cannon boom from where the tide was washing round the caves in the cliffs. When she sat down, supported by the solid earth, her eye met the cliff half-way up its height, she felt safe.

"Do be careful," she called out to Mr Robinson, who was

27

standing on the extreme edge and taking in the view. He ignored her. Had he held her arm she would have been glad to stand beside him and assimilate the grandeur of the view, but she would not—in his present mood—ask for that support, and to look down that distance with no rail to lean upon would make her giddy. She settled herself comfortably on the rug, leaned back against the side of the grassy hollow, and lit a cigarette. Mr Robinson, in profile against that background of many coloured rock and sheer blue sky, looked heroic. He took out a pair of binoculars and surveyed the scene. She was impressed by his imperturbability. Michael had never been one to talk merely to pass the time, had rarely opened his lips except to reprove, complain, impart information or demand it, but Michael had been a chatterbox in comparison with her new mysterious friend; obviously a man of moods for whom this happened to be a bad day; his present languor was in such amazing contrast to the feverishness of last evening. Of the two extremes, she preferred today's. She couldn't cope with drama.

He stood on the cliff edge for fully half an hour, then he turned back and seated himself in the hollow, refusing to share the rug, his arms round his knees, his head propped against the bank.

"The tide is going out," he said.

Miss Kelly found nothing to say to that. Now that he was sitting down, she felt lazily content. That padded booming noise from the cliff, the occasional gawp of a seagull, and an occasional child's voice in the distance—all had a soothing effect on her. She had been more strung up than she realised; gratefully she closed her eyes.

When a motor car revving up—one of the other sight seeing parties taking its departure—woke Miss Kelly, she found herself staring into Mr Robinson's face. It was close to her own. She gave a little shriek. He was crouching over her.

"I beg your pardon," she said. "I must have fallen asleep. What time is it?"

"You were only asleep a very little time," he said.

Then he sat down again.

"You gave me quite a fright just now. Why were you staring

28

at me like that? I was taught that it was very rude to stare at anyone."

"You were fast asleep."

"All the more reason."

"I'll be perfectly frank and tell you that I couldn't help myself. Your resemblance to someone else is the most extraordinary thing. I can't get over it. Asleep, you have a peevish look I remember all too well."

"Peevish? I don't like the sound of that one bit."

"As if you were dreaming that someone had the impertinence not to give you your way. You are accustomed to getting your way I should think."

"When I ask for a thing to be done, I like it to be done; but doesn't everyone?"

As this was followed by silence, Miss Kelly decided to change the conversation.

"May I ask if the person I resemble so closely was a relation of yours?"

"My mother."

Acute disappointment was Miss Kelly's first feeling, resentment at having been taken advantage of. She might have made a fool of herself.

"Were you devoted to her?" she asked, really to comfort herself.

"Not a bit, nor was she to me. She was not even devoted to herself. She never acted like a mother. I never knew what it was like to have a mother. Or a father, if it comes to that."

His voice sounded resentful; and because he had identified her with his mother, Miss Kelly had an uncomfortable feeling that the resentment was aimed at her personally. However, she never failed in conventional politeness.

"That's sad, for any child. Mine died when I was six."

"Then at least you haven't any unpleasant memories of her."

"Far from it," Miss Kelly said.

Mr Robinson got up at this point and resumed his inspection of the cliff. He did not seem to be entranced by the view so much as scrutinising its features through his binoculars.

"I'd say there was a powerful current there. Look at that motor-boat."

He spoke as if Miss Kelly was beside him, so she got up and stood cautiously a few feet from the escarpment. There was a gentle grass slope to the edge proper. Who fell here would have to roll fifty feet before going over the edge.

"You can see the strand at the base of Slieve League," he said. "Look down. Don't be frightened. I'll hold you. How high does the tide rise, I wonder? I suppose one could get down there by going round the top of the cliff. We must come back some other day. I'd like to explore. You get a wonderful panoramic view from here, I must say. But I'd like to get closer."

"You are not afraid of heights?"

"I'm not easily frightened."

A second motor car drove away. There was one other now. Its occupants were not to be seen; Miss Kelly felt a sudden return of her noonday unease, even though Mr Robinson looked splendid, and she liked his stern expression, respecting men who didn't try to conciliate her. Michael had been a bully, and she had heard that her father was held in awe as much by his relations as by his employees. He looked very fierce in his portrait. Mr Robinson would not seem out of place in that company. She decided to ask him something about himself. He had, after all, taken her into his confidence about his mother. She didn't like to hear anyone talking like that about his relations; but, then, there was a great deal about Mr Robinson that didn't fit in with her idea of how people ought to behave.

"Isn't the scenery good where you come from?" That was her clever question when he came back again and, this time, lit a small cigar.

"So—so."

"You're Australian, something tells me."

"What could tell you that?"

"I really can't say. You haven't an Australian accent."

"You probably looked in the register."

"I have never been out there. I haven't met many Australians," she hurried on to hide her mortification.

30

"I have lived there for the last thirty years, but I am not an Australian."

"I thought you looked too distinguished, if you can bear a compliment. I *am* glad I was right."

"How utterly ridiculous. You haven't moved with the times, Miss Kelly. I'm Irish, if you want to know. At least, I was born and grew up here. My father's people came originally from somewhere in England, and my mother was English. Truell was her name. Her father was a doctor in Cornwall. Now you know all about me." ("And don't need to be looking me up on the sly," he seemed to suggest.)

She told him then as much about herself. He didn't pretend to pay attention, and got up before she had finished to look at the sea again.

"That's interesting," he said aloud. She joined him to look, having lost faith in her power to impress him by any of her advantages. He thrust the binoculars into her hands.

"Do you see what looks like a piece of wreckage? Only a speck on the water. There. A gull has perched himself on it. Half an hour ago it was on the shingle at the foot of the cliff. Now it has been swept round in a half circle. I'll look again later on to see if it has moved along the coast or travelled out to sea. There are probably several currents down there."

She looked through the field glasses obediently; but couldn't see how the course of a sheet of wood could be of any interest. They resumed their seats; but this time he came beside her on the rug.

"Is your work in some way connected with the sea?" she asked.

"No. I manage a sheep farm."

Miss Kelly's imagination was given enough to feed upon for several minutes. Her mind was easier now that she knew what he did. Large tracts of land covered with sheep swam before her eyes. From their throats issued one enormous Baa.

"I'm retiring at the end of the year."

"And will you settle down in Ireland?"

"No. But I wanted to have a last look at it. I had never been in

Donegal. My father had a cottage up here; he was for ever promising to have me to stay—as a youth, I mean—but never did. I was rather good at golf, and I looked forward to playing with him; but he had always some excuse. I might never get the opportunity again, so I decided to come to Donegal and see what I had missed."

"Where was your father's cottage?"

"In Portnoo."

"That's not far from where we are staying. I could drive you there tomorrow if you would like me to."

"That's very kind of you. I want to see how that wreckage is behaving." He took up the binoculars and leaped to his feet. Miss Kelly would have appreciated a more enthusiastic response to her offer. But he had only one idea in his mind.

"Yes, drifting straight across. But it may run into a cross-current. I'm going to wait here and see."

His excitement was almost childish. She came beside him to show she was ready to enter into the spirit of the game.

"There, look. Out she goes. Take the glasses."

His hands were trembling. "That might end up anywhere. Doesn't it remind *you* of anything?"

Thoroughly bored at last, and rather cross, she handed back the glasses.

"No, it doesn't. I don't see anything very remarkable about it." She felt cheated. A perfect outing, this should have been. Weather, scenery—everything one could hope for. Mr Robinson had scarcely been civil; and now, at the end of the day, he was behaving as if he wasn't quite right in the head.

"How could it?"

"How could *what*?"

"You haven't taken an interest in the currents. They fascinate me. We think of the tide rolling in and out, punching the clocks for the moon's benefit, the most reliable phenomenon in nature, when in fact the sea underneath is alive with these temperamental little fellows, each with a mind of his own. You can't just throw your garbage on the shingle and take for granted that the tide is going to carry it obediently out to sea. It may end up anywhere, or nobody may see a trace of it ever again. You never can tell. You must forgive me, I have been away quite a long time—thirty years—it seems like ten minutes."

Miss Kelly was more than ready to retrieve the afternoon, when he looked pleasant and talked amiably like this. She would like him to take her into his confidence. There was something which prevented his face from being definitely handsome, she decided, not, so far as she could judge, any fault of his features. In his expression, rather. He so seldom looked at one casually. His staring last night was explained by the circumstances, but she had never seen anyone with quite that expression, and he had the habit of looking into the distance, when he seemed to forget his surroundings. Most disconcerting of all was the way he had of looking up under his eyes; then he seemed infinitely remote and cold. She had been subjected to that stare once and had seen it looming when he said "Doesn't it remind *you* of anything?" But at her first show of temper, he took the nasty look off his face at once. Had he, perhaps, been left too much on his own in Perth, Western Australia? Again, a picture of vast acres peopled only with sheep swam before her eyes. She must make allowances. Having acted as châtelaine for her brother since she left school, she had acquired a poise which should enable her to put a man who needed only oiling of his social joints at ease. She had nothing else to do until Cyril came on Friday.

Theirs was now the only car on the hilltop. Should she suggest that it was time to go back? If they went to Glencolumkille now, it would be rather too close to dinner to pack in a country tea. She waited to see if he would make a suggestion. It was very pleasant here; the sun had not gone down; Slieve League, across the narrow water, really impressed her. She was a figure in the foreground of a masterpiece: Mr Robinson and herself alone in a huge seascape. She couldn't have put the thought into words. Mr Robinson took out cigars.

"Do you smoke these?" he asked.

She laughed merrily at the idea of herself with a cigar in her mouth, but she produced a cigarette, which he lit for her, a repetition of last night's near intimacy. They settled on the rug and smoked in silence.

"Tell me about Australia," Miss Kelly said at last.

"There isn't much to tell. I was very busy."

"Was it very lonely?"

"Not particularly. I am not a person who needs much company. There was always someone around. I travelled about quite a lot."

"Had you always wanted to be a sheep farmer?"

"No: The thought never occurred to me. I'd have liked to go on the stage."

"And why didn't you?"

"That's a long story. I did act a bit."

"Acted? In Australia?"

"Ah, no. That was long after."

Miss Kelly waited for Mr Robinson to develop this interesting topic, but he showed no inclination to reminisce further. However, it opened up attractive possibilities. This, after all, was their first excursion and his reticence impressed her rather than otherwise. If it was she who suggested they should make for home, he was nothing loth; there was no hint of gallantry in his manner—he didn't even open the car door for her. Whatever else, she wasn't going to have "any trouble" with Mr Robinson. He was not a lady's man.

She had met stage people very rarely, only rather distinguished ones on visits to Dublin. Artists didn't come her way unless they had achieved a recognised social standing or were the children of her friends and their friends. However short Mr Robinson's acting career might have been, she could only picture him on the stage in a West End play in the leading part. The vision was romantic and reassuring. Reassuring, because it explained his behaviour when he first saw her and that haunted expression. Even though he had spoken hardly at all she had learned—she thought—a great deal about Mr Robinson this afternoon. His extravagant behaviour was the legacy of his theatrical past and his failure as a cavalier the result of lonely years among Australian sheep.

At Carrick he suggested they should stop for refreshment. In London she had stayed at the Ritz, but in her own country a drink with a man, alone in a bar, was an exciting experience. She was uncertain what to ask for, and let him order whiskey—

34

which she didn't care for—because she felt it seemed appropriate to the surroundings.

Her eyes were almost bright; she was approximately lively; this was as close as she had ever got to "seeing life".

At that time of day the bar was almost deserted; one old man in a corner was making a bottle of stout stretch out to its furthest limits. This was his shelter. He gave a respectful bow to the newcomers, and then wriggled back in his corner as if to emphasise that he was taking up as little space as possible. It was Miss Kelly who had elected to come into the bar instead of sitting in the prim lounge of the hotel. She was so seldom where men were. If someone were to let fall an obscenity, it would have crowned her day; but the barman and his familiar customer gave up whatever conversation they were having in deference to the strangers.

"Tell me about your time in the theatre," Miss Kelly said. She had carefully gone over in her mind the range of conversational possibilities so as to avoid bringing on another of his silences.

"It amounted to nothing really. I never had more than a few lines to say. At school, I was better than most at acting, and as I didn't like the idea of examinations, I asked my father to let me study for the stage in London. He wasn't prepared to pay the fees. Then I met someone who was acting with a group who had got up a company in Dublin. He introduced me to the man who was running the theatre. I was there for about a year."

"I might have seen you. I might well have. I used to go to the theatre quite a lot, whenever we came up to Dublin. In those days, people who lived in the country made Thursday their day. It used to be quite fun. The club at lunchtime was full of people one knew."

"I don't think they would have had much time for the Phoenix Theatre, somehow."

"But I remember the Phoenix Theatre very well. It was such a pity it couldn't carry on. Maurice Elvery was a marvellous actor, even if he was a little plump and elderly for some of his parts. I remember him in *Ghosts*. He was wonderful. He did all those Chekhov plays: *Cherry Orchard*, *Seagull*, *A Doll's House*. Or is *A*

35

Doll's House by Ibsen? I am always getting them mixed up."

"I was to have a part in *The Seagull*. It was my first break. But I wasn't cut out for the stage."

"I can't agree. When I saw you last night for the first time, I thought you looked very like an actor."

"That hardly counts."

"What happened? Why did you not play the part? Did you get ill? I shouldn't ask so many questions."

"You might say I got ill. Do you want another? Or shall we be moving along."

Miss Kelly did not want any more whiskey; she would have submitted if she thought it would keep the conversation afloat; but she recognised Mr Robinson's symptoms. He was in one of his moods again. She had upset him. He was impossibly touchy. In the car she pretended nothing was amiss and chatted away about Cyril. If Mr Robinson stayed on for a few extra days, he would meet Cyril. He would like him, find him amusing. "Unless you dislike that type. He's nice as can be, but when you meet him you'll see what I mean. He gives the most perfect dinner parties and he has a devoted housekeeper—Mrs *Robinson*, I've just remembered. What an amusing coincidence."

"Where do you live?"

"In Swords, between Malahide and Donabate, at the estuary. Rathbeg, the house is called. Are you familiar with that part of the country?"

Miss Kelly was accustomed to silence when she expected a reply from Mr Robinson, and he had never made any pretence of interest when she talked about herself. He was self-centred, she had decided; but what else would anyone be who lived for thirty years among sheep? She didn't take offence therefore when he made no reply to her question, but drove on and waited for him to renew the conversation. It was only by chance, when she thought she had missed the road and pulled up, that she noticed his face had lost all its colour.

"Is anything the matter? You don't look well, Mr Robinson."

"I'm all right. Please don't bother about me."

Anxiously, taking fleeting glances at him from time to time, she hurried home. When they arrived at the guest house, he had regained his complexion, but he hurried in, and muttered some excuse when he left her in the hall and went to his room. She had thought he might possibly invite her to join him at dinner, and wondered if he did should she accept the invitation. She knew what Michael would have said. But Michael died fifteen years ago, and she was fifty-two and it was time she stopped listening to that voice from beyond the grave. Her concern for propriety was laughable, she told herself. Nobody would take the slightest notice, or gossip, or care. She must get what she could out of life. She waited downstairs. When he hadn't appeared at half-past eight, she went into dinner alone. Should she enquire about him? Was it right to leave him up there alone after that strange fit or faint or whatever it was in the car? He did look better when they came in. His eyes had a very peculiar glazed appearance, but he had got back his colour. On balance she decided to leave him alone this evening. In the morning, if he didn't appear, she would talk to the proprietor's wife. She would know what to do.

Would he take her up on her offer to drive him to Portnoo tomorrow, if he was himself again? Could she put up with another outing like today's, such unsatisfactory behaviour, such oddness and near rudeness? She decided that, on the whole, she could.

III

Mr Robinson was busy at breakfast and did not see Miss Kelly come in. Should she go at once to his table to enquire after his health? Her hesitation was apparent to anyone who was watching the development of this comedy. She decided not to. In due course, she would catch his attention from her proper place and wave a cheery greeting. Her attempts at lightness were heroic. Mr Robinson, since she had met him, had not smiled once nor made any attempt at a pleasantry. Were it not for his mysteriousness, Miss Kelly would have had to vote him the least rewarding of all her acquaintances. How Cyril would have laughed and chattered and gossiped had he been here; and yet she would not have had him in Mr Robinson's place. She was romantic, she decided. She must be. Why had she only discovered that now, and what was there about Mr Robinson that had brought this out? He had done nothing to please her; his manner left everything to be desired, and yet the time since he arrived had been enthralling in a manner quite outside her experience. At winter sports in Switzerland, when she was young, a handsome skiing instructor had paid her flattering attention; and for a year or two, whenever there was frost and sunshine together, his kiss in a chalet on the slopes burned again on her lips. It was the high point of that holiday. That had been a romantic moment, certainly. At seventeen. All the girls were after him. When she asked herself after a suitor withdrew if there was something missing in her that she couldn't lose her head over any man, she reminded herself of that kiss.

The attraction of the Austrian skiing instructor required no explanation; Mr Robinson's disturbed her; for once she couldn't understand herself or predict what she might do in unseen circumstances. She had pondered long over his sudden sickness or whatever it was—following, as she remembered, her description of her house. How could that have upset him? Possibly, he was subject to recurrent attacks; the result of malaria perhaps (the idea of his rolling about in an epileptic fit was too horrible to contemplate).

"May I interrupt you for a moment?" Mr Robinson was at her elbow. His manner had entirely changed. He sounded conciliatory, almost obsequious.

"Don't let me interrupt your breakfast. I think you did say yesterday that you were on for a visit to Portnoo; have you thought about it since? Will it be a bore for you? Please say. I can hire a car for the day, but if I have to, I should do something about it now."

Miss Kelly had only one way of expressing herself. It disguised her girlish excitement unless he noticed her heightened colour.

"I was looking forward to our trip; and the weather is behaving beautifully."

"You are quite sure. Well, that settles it. I see they pack lunch-baskets here—I should have given notice yesterday—but I expect I could persuade them to put up something. Unless you would prefer to lunch in an hotel. There's one in Portnoo, I know. I looked it up."

"A picnic would be much more fun but I must pay my share, unless you would let me order the lunch, and you can contribute something for us to drink. Isn't that a better arrangement?"

"This is my treat. I insist. You are supplying the transport."

Miss Kelly, who was never indifferent to financial arrangements, however trivial, saw the force of this.

"Perhaps they will put their best foot forward for a man. Tell me when you would like to start."

In half an hour they were under way. It was all very unlike yesterday. When she enquired solicitously, Mr Robinson refused to admit that he had been unwell.

"I get tired. I find the climate here relaxing. I can't keep my eyes open most of the time." He gave her no opportunity to pursue the point. He wouldn't stop talking.

"I wonder if we will find the cottage: 'Peggy's Leg', he called it, after a sort of candy he used to eat as a child. Bullseyes, liquorice allsorts. I don't suppose they exist today. I daresay

39

whoever came after him changed the name. It was quite innocent in his time; but even so, a rather frivolous ploy, don't you think, for a lawyer living apart from his wife? They separated when I was a child. Nobody could have lived with my mother. I know. I tried. My father kept a housekeeper in his Dublin house; she used to look after me. I went to a run-down school, where I learned nothing, until I was old enough to be sent to England."

"What school did you go to?" Miss Kelly set store by public schools. They helped her to place people.

"It was very obscure. I wasn't really up to standard. I hated school, and the headmaster wrote to my father to take me away when I couldn't get out of the lower forms. In those days there wasn't the same pressure as there would be now. I wouldn't have got in, even to such a second-rate school. I had a good tenor voice and I was passable at games, but I couldn't concentrate on lessons. My father used to get depressed by my reports. I was fond of him and I'd have liked to please him; but he couldn't communicate with me. I did everything I could to attract his attention, even swallowed all his sleeping pills. It nearly killed me. He sent me to a psychiatrist. I don't know what he discovered; but it led to my being handed over to my mother. I was about fourteen. I got special coaching then with the idea of sending me to Trinity. But I couldn't concentrate. I wanted to go on the stage. I told you about that, didn't I?

"My mother told me that my father gave me up because he had a woman in tow. She said she had to leave him because he was always in pursuit of women. I never saw any round the place when I lived with him. He often told me my mother was mad. I saw him sometimes. But he never knew how to talk to me. He'd give me money, and when he bought this cottage we are going to look for, he kept on—as I told you—holding out hopes of a visit. Somehow, my mother got hold of the information that the place was called Peggy's Leg. I used to hear her laughing to her friends over the telephone about it. She never minded what she said about him. But she knew I objected to it, and she only indulged herself when she was having a row with me. 'You're the image of your father', was one of her favourite expressions. He was rather close about money; she had quite a lot of her own and a house. I suppose he thought she could afford to keep me. When I wanted to go to RADA he said it was nonsense and an excuse to escape work. He couldn't imagine anyone belonging to him actually living out of art. We were not that sort of family. My mother was quite keen on the idea, but not to the extent of paying for it. When I met this friend I told you about who was acting at the Phoenix Theatre, she raised no objection. Maybe because she knew my father wouldn't approve. She would do anything she could to vex him.

"I don't believe he kept a woman up here; as I used to hear her say. Apart from any other consideration, it would have been bad for a solicitor's business in those days. Appearances still counted, and Portnoo, I understand, was quite a favourite place for holiday homes. He would have run into clients—that would have been awkward for him. It was just a place to escape to, I expect. If only he had kept his promise, we might have become friends. But he never got over my trying to kill myself. He was uneasy when I was with him, couldn't get rid of me fast enough.

"I could never get him to talk even about family matters. When I went to live with my mother, he gave up abusing her to my face. When I called on him for money, as I did from time to time, he'd say 'Why don't you ask that mother of yours? She's stuffed with money. I've none.' He had to pay her an allowance and run a second house on the income from a very small practice. Never made more than a thousand a year. Paid his head clerk three pounds a week and the junior thirty shillings. Can you believe it? No wonder he thought the thirty shillings a week he allowed me princely. When my mother drove me out of her house, she added a pound to that. It was all I had to live on."

As if he had bored himself, Mr Robinson stopped suddenly and gave an ugly yawn. Miss Kelly waited, and then decided that he intended to give her an innings. She needed time to assimilate the information he had poured out. A solicitor with a small practice married to a wife with some money of her own: that set the scene. He had jibbed at telling her the name of the school; she had never heard of any so obscure that it was indecent to mention in public. Her Irish friends, on the whole,

41

had gone to the Benedictine and Jesuit schools in England; but she had assumed Mr Robinson was not a Catholic, and if he couldn't confront her with one of the historic names, it was a tribute to his discernment that he didn't come out with some place she had never heard of. This was the part of his story that she had no difficulty in grasping; her experience did not help her to assimilate the rest so easily. She couldn't imagine circumstances so unhappy as he had related; at first they had alienated her as people always did when she couldn't fit them into her own mould. A sense of remoteness constituted her sympathy. She felt she must be organically different from the sort of person who tried to live on £1,000 a year. When Mr Robinson was young that meant, of course, five times as much as it did today.

"How dreadful for you. I know *exactly* how you must have felt. My parents died when I was quite a child; but I had an old aunt, rather a martinet, my father's eldest sister, she used to come to stay with us, and there were endless rows between her and my brother. He—"

"Stop when we come to those houses. I have an idea that Father's cottage was on this side of the village, near the golf links." Mr Robinson had not been listening, and Miss Kelly was not offended; she had merely returned the conversational ball, as she was accustomed. She had nothing to tell about Aunt Jane, other than that she was consistently disagreeable. She stopped the car, and Mr Robinson got out and looked about him. There were a few small, nondescript houses on the roadside, and, stretching out to the right, a long gleaming strand.

He got in again.

"Stop at a garage. I can enquire from the man who gives us petrol. I don't want to make ourselves conspicuous, you understand."

A garage was discovered just round the next corner, but the boy in charge of petrol had never heard of a cottage with that name.

The post office seemed the obvious port of call; it was in the only large store in the village, but Mr Robinson became tongue-tied when he began to put the question, and bought a pound's worth of stamps instead. Miss Kelly saw an opportunity to be helpful.

"We were looking for a cottage. It used to be called Peggy's Leg," she said to the woman behind the counter.

"I never heard of it: but there's been a lot of building round here, this last few years."

"Oh, this is an old cottage."

"I'll ask my husband. He may know. He has lived here longer than myself."

When Miss Kelly looked up for approval, she met a face of rage.

"Why are you drawing attention to us like that? What possessed you?"

She was mortified. The friendly woman hadn't even smiled at the name. It was really impossible to please Mr Robinson.

The proprietor of the shop now came forward to say he had never heard of the cottage; who was the owner? He would certainly be able to trace the house if he knew that.

"I'm afraid we don't know. It isn't of the least importance. May I buy that box of shortbread; how much is it?" Miss Kelly couldn't hide her agitation.

"It's not a name you'd forget," the shop man said as he handed back the change for the notes she pulled frantically out of her purse. He smiled at her, turned his head to wink at the gentleman, and thought better of it.

Outside, Miss Kelly turned on Mr Robinson. "I'm very sorry; but really I can't see why we need to be so mysterious. It's quite natural that you should want to see your father's house. That man would have understood; he seemed a friendly sort of person."

"I'd be very much obliged in future if you didn't try to manage my business for me. I am perfectly capable of looking after it myself."

"I had no intention of managing your business. I thought we were merely looking for a cottage. If you would prefer to look round on your own, I'll take a drive and come back here whenever you say."

"Why would you do that?"

"I don't want to be abused and attacked. I came out for pleasure."

"Nobody is abusing or attacking you. I'm sorry if I was short with you just then, but I'm used to doing things my own way."

Miss Kelly swallowed her wrath. So was she. A large part of Mr Robinson's attraction lay in his not letting her. He was unwell. That explained his changes of mood. She must humour him like a child.

"We can walk about; we have all day; it's a pretty place."

He looked disproportionately relieved, she thought, as if they had passed through some crisis, instead of quarrelling over nothing at all, as it seemed to her.

She walked obediently beside him; they traversed the golf-links, strolled down the pier, followed a road on which there were a good many houses, most of them recently built.

"The name may not be written up."

He let her observation pass. He was beginning to lose interest. She could always see when this was happening. When he was on a trail he was like a hound on a leash, then, quite suddenly, he went slack and looked aimlessly round him. It was, she decided, the moment to suggest their picnic.

"I want to call in at the hotel for a moment," she said, "and you must decide where we will take our lunch."

In the washroom, she looked at her face in the mirror. She was shocked by what she saw, and looked again. Her face changed as little and as slowly as her life; there were crow's feet round her eyes, but as light as could be, and an almost imperceptible droop at one corner of her mouth. Fortunately, she hadn't that rose petal complexion which suffers the same fate as roses. Her cheekbones (like Mr Robinson's) were high, the skin taut. Her neck—the most tell-tale place—showed a slight slackening, perhaps. But she was not looking at the too familiar features, what arrested her was a new look, an almost furtive look in her eyes. She had never seen it there before today. She was looking at someone she didn't know.

That Mr Robinson would follow her example and come into the

44

hotel, she had taken for granted; but she was surprised to find him waiting for her in the hall. She expected to meet him at the car, parked—with forethought—outside. There was nothing unusual in what he did. For most couples it would have been the natural place to meet; but something told her that he had waited there to prevent her from asking questions at the desk. His manner, however, was genial for him.

"We might as well drive around until we see a likely spot."

"And you can keep your eyes skinned in case we pass the cottage." She was responding to his better temper, but she couldn't keep up with Mr Robinson. He turned his face away from the window.

"I don't think it's here at all."

"But how . . ."

"It was so long ago."

"It may have been pulled down?"

"I don't know if it ever existed."

"But your father invited you to come and stay there."

"Forget it. I don't want to think about it any more."

Miss Kelly was a literal person; she found this complete change of plan incomprehensible; but she was more than pleased to throw up the search and concentrate on the picnic.

She drove haphazardly, coming back towards the coast whenever the road led them inland. He gave the signal to stop when they had travelled about ten miles. They had reached an inlet of the sea with a strand that looked like brown sugar—and not a soul in sight. Miss Kelly decided where they should sit and laid out the fare, giving little cries of satisfaction. Lobster! My goodness! When Mr Robinson produced a bottle of champagne, the transformation of the day was complete. Miss Kelly had a large appetite, and did justice to the food.

"Go on. Eat up. I'm famished," she said. There was nothing over-refined about her attitude to nourishment, and the champagne in the sun acted quickly. She lay back, closed her eyes, and listened to the murmur of the tide.

As once before when she opened her eyes, she looked into Mr Robinson's face, but this time she was not frightened. She smiled up at him. "I drank far too much."

Did he want to kiss her? She wanted him to kiss her; she was quite certain of that. She would make a formal protest and submit. Being kissed by Mr Robinson would be a shattering experience, she decided. The furtive look she had seen in her eyes in the hotel glass told her that she had been preparing all day for this. Had she not been, she would most certainly have gone home after the shop incident. Nobody in all her life had ever dared to speak to her like that. She had never felt like this before. She must be in love with Mr Robinson.

"Your eyes are not the same colour. Hers were flecked with brown," he said.

Then he sat down, quite close to Miss Kelly. He had put off his distrait manner. The champagne had not made him merry or, apparently, flirtatious, but it had had some tonic effect. She wished she could do or say something to impress him; but he never showed any interest in what she said. He was enormously self-centred, she decided; but so were most of the men she knew, and any she had found attractive. She reached out a hand and touched his sleeve and waited. Then, when he did not grasp it, she pretended to be signalling her intention of saying something important. It meant a change of mood that was quite artificial; but she was rescuing her pride.

"May I ask you a question? It is rather personal, but I shall be uneasy in my mind until I clear it up?"

Mr Robinson seemed to consider; then he said, not encouragingly, "What is it?"

"You remember when we were on our way home yesterday, after I told you where my house was, you suddenly became pale and silent and looked really ill. I was quite frightened. Do you think you ought to see a doctor? You are a very highly-strung person, and I am sure you need some sort of tranquilliser. You said just now that you might be only imagining what you told me about your father's cottage. Isn't that serious, if you really don't remember? You ought to get medical help. I know I've no right to talk to you like this; but it seems to me that you are putting an unnecessary strain on yourself. We've known each other for such a short time." She stopped; she felt a jerk in her throat: the champagne was going to her head.

"I think you exaggerate. I'm exceptionally tough, let me tell you. But I'm accustomed to living alone, and in the ordinary course, I don't have to consider anyone else's moods or fancies. I will satisfy your curiosity—"

"Oh, *please*. I am not curious."

"You mean, you are not inquisitive. I'm sure you're not; but I think I owe you an explanation of my manner this morning. I regret my rudeness."

"You weren't rude exactly . . ."

"Yes. I was. I must explain that my past life in Ireland has become so like a dream in retrospect that I am never quite sure what is fact and what I imagine. When I saw you, I did really think it was my mother. I didn't say to myself, as anyone else would have: 'That's extraordinarily like'. I never doubted it was her. In the same way, my contacts with my father were so full of frustrations that I can't be certain from one moment to the next how much of my recollection is only a day-dream remembered. I used to day-dream more than most people. It was the reason why I couldn't study. I was averagely intelligent, but I would never undertake to give an accurate account of anything that happened in the past, especially towards the end; from the time my mother threw me out, to be precise, because it was after that I read a book which had an extraordinary effect on me. Believe me, Miss Kelly, when people talk about censorship, and I hear them argue that a book can't influence people's conduct, I want to tear them apart. That book took me over so completely that I was never certain whether I was acting in my own life, or as a character in the novel. I identified so closely with the hero, I called him by my name. That's odd, wouldn't you say? You might understand me identifying with him. Lots of young people do with film actors, book characters, pop stars, and all the rest; but I never heard of people who thought their hero identified with them. It's rather egotistic, I suppose. But I was fond of my father. I was sorry for him, and even at the end I wished he could have known I took the sleeping-tablets to make him notice me. But there are times when I don't really believe anyone else exists in the world except as fictional characters, as if my whole life were a play or novel. In this case, the novel was

47

made into a play. I read it when I was watching the rehearsals, and they helped to bring it alive in one sense; but when I was watching the play on the stage, I saw myself up there. The actor in the leading part was acting me. I was on stage. Then something even stranger happened. The ordinary sequence of time no longer existed for me. Things began to happen in their wrong order."

"I don't understand."

"You must try to imagine me living two separate lives, as myself and as the character in this novel. Right? Sometimes things that happened in the novel started to happen to me, but not necessarily in the order in which they occurred in the novel (or in the play, for that matter. They had become indistinguishable). For instance, the hero has a frightful dream. I had that dream, exactly, in every detail. But what was much more extraordinary—I don't expect you to believe this—but as I have told you so much, you might as well hear this as well. I told you that a friend was responsible for bringing me into the theatre. I met him through my mother, of all people. He was a friend of one of the women friends she played golf and bridge with. One of these women was always talking about a strange young man who helped her with interior decoration, advised her about pets, was full of hints about cooking, and the garden. A genius. I happened to call on this woman, when she was out, with a message from my mother, and I met this marvel. He was dyeing her bedroom curtains a nice shade of green when I called. He took to me at once, invited me to stay for tea, made me feel important for the first time in my life, wanted to know what I did. When I said my father wouldn't pay my RADA fees, he said it was criminal. I was perfectly equipped for the stage; he asked me to walk about so that he could view me properly. He ran his hands over me. I didn't like that; but I assumed it was a trick of the trade. He wasn't like any man I'd ever met. I didn't know very much, you must believe me. I didn't mix with other children. I got on all right at school, but I was never close to anyone. I never wanted to be. There didn't seem to be a place for anyone else in my private world. Used you to day-dream, Miss Kelly?"

"Well. I suppose everyone—" she began.

"I couldn't make him out," Mr Robinson continued, "but he was obviously delighted with me. When I got home I told my mother about him—well, not everything. I wanted her to know that I could impress people. 'Oh, that cissy', was all she said. Nobody had ever made so much of me before. I didn't tell her that he had invited me to have tea in his flat. He had a magnificent tea laid out when I arrived, like something in a coloured advertisement; honey, scones, sandwiches, fruit cake, some special brand of tea. He showed me his collection of neckties and insisted on giving me two, and wrote my name in a book of poems he had had privately printed, signing himself my 'affectionate friend'; and he told me, whenever I could, to present my left profile; it was handsomer than my right. He had spoken to Maurice Elvery about me, he said, and I was to go for an audition at the theatre, but before that he wanted to coach me. He went to no end of trouble, selecting speeches out of plays for me to learn by heart. I was to come back in a week's time, when I had learned the speeches and recite them to him; then we would have dinner."

"And did you?" Miss Kelly was only prompting Mr Robinson who had been silent for a whole minute. She felt sure she was going to hear something that would upset her but she would be much more upset if she didn't hear it.

When he didn't answer, she sat up and looked at Mr Robinson. He was quite oblivious of her, and was examining his hands as if, while he was busy talking, someone might have stolen a fingernail.

"Mr Robinson: are you feeling all right?"

He seemed to shake himself out of a daze.

"What time is it? Was I asleep for long?"

"A minute at the most."

"I beg your pardon. Lunch in the fresh air. I suppose we might as well be on our way. I haven't the least idea where we are."

"I can show you the map. Do we have to go? I was so interested . . ." But Mr Robinson wasn't listening. He was packing the remains of lunch with complete concentration. On the journey home, she asked in what she intended to be a casual tone, what happened to his friend.

"He married. A widow. Stuffed with money. They had a house in Hertfordshire and a villa near Florence. She was old enough to be his mother. I expect he's dead by now."

"He was much older than you?"

"You couldn't tell what age he was. I thought of him as some kind of bird; he dressed in bright colours; he had the hard bright eyes of a bird, and his nose and chin always reminded me of a parrot's beak. He had a screeching laugh."

"I know the type so well."

"I hope you keep your hand on your purse then. He had no conscience about money. I had my first blazing row with my mother when he took a ten pound note out of her dressing-table drawer. She accused me of the theft."

"Was that when she put you out of the house?"

"No. That was something else that came later."

"But you were very fond of your friend."

"I don't know what you mean by 'friend'." He sounded quite sharp, and Miss Kelly was thrown into confusion. She tried to cover it by lighting a cigarette for herself. On this occasion, he didn't offer to help; he was staring out of his window at the scenery; and there was nothing encouraging about the line of his jaw.

She was in one of the situations in which she missed somebody to consult with; she had no experience of dealing with people who got off the rails; there were oddities in her family and among her acquaintances, but their eccentricity was accepted and manifest, like the colour of their hair. One didn't have to adapt oneself to them. This was when Miss Kelly needed Aggie; Aggie would have listened. Why wasn't she here?

Mr Robinson was leaving tomorrow. It was a relief, in a way; but she had an unsatisfied feeling that an opportunity had been lost; for some reason she had failed to draw out the heart of his mystery. He had started to confide in her and roused her curiosity and then, apparently, decided to become cautious. He never mentioned names, she noticed, after the first night when he thought she was his mother. At the recollection of this she nearly laughed aloud. It was so absurd. If she tried to tell Cyril, he would pull her leg about it for weeks. She would be quite unable to convey the force of Mr Robinson's personality. He wasn't like anyone she had ever heard of, much less met.

And she was piqued at the thought that he would go away and leave her so very little wiser. There was very little time now. Should she invite him to dine at her table? It was his last evening; he had provided lunch; it would be merely polite.

She longed to, but was fearful that he might pretend not to hear or choose some other way to mortify her. Had he noticed her hand on his sleeve? Did he see it as an invitation? If so, he might have thought she had designs on him. Meanwhile, they were approaching the guest house.

"Well," she said, drawing up on the side of the gravel sweep, "that was a pleasant outing."

Mr Robinson did not choose to second that. He said they must not forget to return the lunch basket. He was clearly not in a mood to encourage fulsomeness. Rebuffed, Miss Kelly let herself out—Mr Robinson didn't open car doors—and she didn't even wait for him, but walked across the gravel, letting him follow with the basket. Indoors, she was hailed by the proprietor's wife.

"Oh, Miss Kelly, you have just missed a telephone call. A Mr Forbes. He said would you ring him up when you came in?"

"That's Cyril," Miss Kelly explained to Mr Robinson. "I hope nothing's the matter with *him*," and to the woman at the telephone, "I'll take the call in my bedroom, if you would be so good as to get me the number—Killiney 831999."

"You'll excuse me," Miss Kelly said to Mr Robinson. She was grateful to Cyril for providing her with an exit line. She was not going to make any more overtures to Mr Robinson. Let him approach her if he wanted to see her again before he went away. She would behave as if he wasn't there.

Cyril was merely being fussy, recapitulating the arrangements. He would take the Friday morning train to Bundoran, and she would meet him at the station.

"How are you getting on up there? Is your throat better?

51

Mind you don't get into any mischief when I'm not around to look after you."

Cyril, bright as a bee, firing off questions, never waiting for answers. "They'll come of their own accord if they're important." What a contrast to Mr Robinson with his glooms, his silences, his awful temper; and yet she took little comfort from the assurance that Cyril was on his way. If Mr Robinson were to call her in her room and invite her to dinner. . . . She could think of nothing else. The telephone rang once. It rang again. Miss Kelly was afraid to pick up the receiver. Then she lifted it with elaborate slowness. She could sense Mr Robinson's presence before he spoke.

"Miss Kelly. This is Henry Robinson. Would you like to join me for dinner this evening?"

She paused, counted three to herself, and then said, "That's very kind of you. I was going to be alone."

"I'll meet you downstairs then. About seven-thirty?"

He cut off at once.

Miss Kelly sat on her bed for five minutes without moving. Then she looked down and saw the telephone receiver was in her lap. She called herself to order. It was six o'clock. She would take a long, deep, comfortable bath, then dress very slowly, and feel utterly relaxed when she joined Mr Robinson at the bar.

Half a bottle of champagne at lunchtime had pleasantly gone to her head. She must be careful. Drink made her apologetic, and inclined to be silly. Not that she often took too much; but sometimes it happened, when she wasn't paying attention. It didn't show her at her best; she lost her poise. She had this image of herself as a queenly personage. Mr Robinson would offer her something to drink before dinner. That would be as it should be. Two glasses of wine at dinner. Not more. And no brandy or liqueurs afterwards—or one, at most, if she felt she needed it.

The unfamiliar expression in her eye—it was in the right eye—before lunch wasn't there any more when she looked in her glass; and her body in the bath, where it seemed to float under the water, reminded her of the edge of the surf she had been

staring at while Mr Robinson talked in the afternoon . . . sea-
weed too, the kind like grass. Had it a special name? She had
mixed bath essence in the water, she lay in the foam; now only
her breasts could be seen. They were round and firm. If she had
had children, they might look like empty hot-water bottles.
What did men think about these things? How could any
man—how could any woman, rather, allow a man to see her if
she got like that? How much in fact, did married people *see* of
each other? She had no idea. She didn't know what was happening around her. Never had to, really. And preferred not to think
about it. Mr Robinson's description of his actor friend seemed
to promise the kind of unpleasantness she avoided, but he did
say he was young at the time and didn't know about these
things; and there were men like Cyril, who was perfectly nice,
and innocuous, and seemed satisfied to live for parties and
being friends with everyone. Nothing sinister went on in
Cyril's lovely home. It was kept in such perfect condition.
His temperament made him much easier to talk to than the
ordinary man, and he didn't seem to mind what age women
were. That made him a treasure when someone antediluvian
had to be entertained. He played them up like anything.
Essentially kind.

Mr Robinson's friend didn't sound at all like that; and
hadn't he made it plain that he was a thief? Mr Robinson's
revelations tended to the sinister. It was a wonder that he had
come back, even to take a last look at a country which had
such disagreeable associations for him. What was this mystery about his father? Why, having gone into such detail
about his cottage—its silly name etc.—had Mr Robinson suddenly thrown up the search and said it was probably all
make-believe? When he went on and on about the play or
novel or whatever it was that had affected him so strongly,
she hadn't been able to follow him at all. There was something very strange about Mr Robinson, and yet he had this
fascination for her. "Turned her on"—that's what Cyril
would say when she told him. He would make capital out of
her story, if she let him, tease her no end. He was a frightful
tease.

She had never washed herself so thoroughly or scented and powdered herself afterwards with such care or looked so long in the glass before she decided eventually to wear the plain white silk blouse over her black skirt; but, even with all the time she took bathing and dressing, there was still half an hour to put in. She lit a cigarette and turned on the radio. Someone was reading fat stock prices.

IV

MR ROBINSON WAS in the hall, looking anxious. He came forward in a fussy way, as if she had kept him waiting.

"We might as well go to our table," he said, "unless you want a drink."

It was not as she had pictured it would be; her appearance seemed to make no impression on him; he never looked at her, but turned away at once when she agreed enthusiastically to their sitting down at once. She beamed round the room when they were seated and gave the menu attention it hardly deserved in an effort to create a party atmosphere; but Mr Robinson was in a hurry to dispose of the preliminaries.

"Would you like claret, if you're having beef?" he said, and had ordered a bottle before she had time to consider the suggestion. What now was on his mind?

He made no effort to hide his impatience with the waitress when she was serving them, and had refused the first course before he recollected himself and called her back. He snapped at her then and watched to make sure she had gone away before he settled down. There was nothing vague or wandering about his manner now. His eyes looked troubled, and Miss Kelly bade farewell to her hopes for the evening.

"You were very good to agree to this," he said. "I wanted particularly to talk to you tonight. I may not get an opportunity in the morning. When we were coming in after our drive, I couldn't help hearing the woman at the telephone saying that someone called Forbes was calling you. You told me his name was Cyril. I connected the two in my mind with someone I knew, and when you gave a Killiney telephone number, I felt quite certain. Is this Cyril Forbes a man of about my own age? His parents were very wealthy; he was an only child; they gave rather grand entertainments?"

"That's Cyril. He hasn't changed, and never will. His mother was a spoilt beauty. She had the money; she used to keep her husband and Cyril on red-hot coals, threatening to change her will whenever one of them annoyed her."

Mr Robinson made the fly-brushing gesture Miss Kelly had learned to recognise. He never welcomed more information than he was looking for. He wouldn't allow her to make herself interesting.

"I think you said he was coming to stay here?"

"That's why he rang up. Cyril's very fussy about his arrangements. I'm to meet him on Friday. He will stay over the weekend. I'm having friends to dinner on Saturday. I wish you could be there. Must you really go so soon? I am out to dinner quite a lot during the next few days. I have friends who live here that I met through Cyril. I know you'd like them."

Mr Robinson made a slight grimace. Then he leaned forward.

"I am going to make what you may think an odd request, but will you promise not to talk about me to Cyril Forbes? I've nothing against him, and we scarcely knew each other. I used to hear about the grand parties at second-hand, you understand. But he may give you a wrong impression about me. I've suffered a great deal. I've been unwell. Coming back to this country has put me under more strain than I could ever have imagined. You may have noticed I was preoccupied at times. That friend of mine—why do I call him friend?—used to go to the Forbes' parties. He liked to be asked out by rich people; he was on his best behaviour. But he fell out with most of them because he couldn't keep his hands off things. He told lies, pretending he wanted them for some childish or sentimental reason, and if he wasn't made a present, he offered to buy. Pieces were traced afterwards to antique shops—he couldn't keep out of them—or auctions. I think his friendship with the Forbeses ended over a Florentine bronze that he said he wanted as a paper-weight. It was a museum piece."

"But I'm sure Cyril won't connect you with that, and after how many years? I won't mention this person. I promise. Anyhow, you never told me his name."

"I don't want you to mention my name to your friend. I've

56

suffered too much from falsehoods in the past. I've gone through very bad times. A man like Cyril Forbes, who has never even boiled a kettle for himself, is quite incapable of understanding what life can be like when the world goes against you."

Miss Kelly welcomed the rôle of comforter. Cyril, she reassured Mr Robinson, was more compassionate and sympathetic than most people realised, the very last person to spread nasty rumours, although addicted to gossip, certainly, but only light-heartedly, never to wound. Mr Robinson was plainly uninterested.

"I want you to promise not to mention anything I've told you to Cyril Forbes."

"Very well. If you say so. I can hold my tongue."

Mr Robinson uncrumpled visibly. The anxiety in his eyes faded out gradually, as when a television set is switched off. Impatient of interruption when he was in possession of conversation, when he had had his say his manner implied that there was nothing further to discuss. Miss Kelly's efforts to set up happier topics met with unappreciative nods; but she kept her smile on and rattled away. She had watched married couples in hotels; in many cases, particularly at breakfast, she noticed that the wife did all the talking. Husbands, she decided, did theirs in bed, if they talked at all. But she was not married to Mr Robinson; he was her host; he should have made more effort.

There was frost in the air; after dinner there would be no sitting out. In the drawing-rooms, every word said would be heard, and even though Miss Kelly's conversation could have been broadcast through a microphone without offence, she had looked forward to something less banal at their last meeting.

Some thoughts of the same order must have been going through Mr Robinson's mind. She was surprised when they had finished coffee (she had refused brandy) to hear him say, "I'd ask you to come and sit in my room, but it isn't comfortable."

"We can use mine."

She astonished herself. But the words were spoken. "It's Number 7. I'll slip up in front of you, if you don't mind, and make sure it's habitable."

She lacked nerve to walk upstairs with Mr Robinson.

"I'll get something sent up," he said. "What do you fancy?"

"Brandy," Miss Kelly said.

Her room was pleasant; a large window commanded the best view. There were two comfortable armchairs. When Mr Robinson knocked on the door, she had arranged them to her satisfaction, not too close, and facing the window.

When Mr Robinson came in he was wearing carpet slippers and carried a box. He might have been any respectable family man, making preparations for Christmas. The box was the lubricant the situation required. Miss Kelly had never entertained in her room unless she was ill; and none of the clichés she had on hand for conversational openings seemed to fit the occasion comfortably. She concentrated on the box. "What have you there? I must see? Let me guess."

It was a cardboard box that had seen much wear and held no promise of champagne or slippers. Mr Robinson might have been presenting his niece with a pet rabbit. And his niece would have comported herself in much the same manner.

"I thought you might like a game of chess," Mr Robinson said.

"I can't play. What a pity!" Miss Kelly's heart began to beat more regularly. The temperature of the room had not fallen; but she put a match to the fire that was set in the grate. It seemed appropriate. Mr Robinson, who had begun to unpack his set, put it away. He looked rueful, as one does when not called on to display an accomplishment.

"I never learned. It required too much concentration. I've begun to play bridge. Everyone did when I was growing up; but television changed all that. Have you television in Australia? Is your chair quite comfortable, by the way? You don't *look* comfortable. Would you prefer to sit on this side?"

"It'll do very well," Mr Robinson said. "I like chess. Always did. I get a magazine which has chess problems, and I work them out. There was a man who worked with me—a Czech—we used to play chess every evening. He usually beat me, and I'll tell you why: he never got rattled, nothing upset his concentration. Mine is rattled by the least thing. I must have perfect quiet.

Anyone can upset me who wants to. You may have noticed. I can't bear even to be watched for long. An audience puts me off. I can never understand how married couples put up with it."

"Put up with what, Mr Robinson?"

"Being watched—being watched by each other from the time they get up until the time they go to bed, being watched in bed until they get up in the morning to be watched again. Every move of every muscle being watched. It would drive me mad."

"Some people are too possessive. I think it's a great mistake. No matter how much one likes a person, there are times when one wants to be on one's own. I do understand exactly how you feel."

"But they are watching you all the same. 'Where is he?' 'What is he doing?' 'Why did he say that?' 'Who is he with?' It never stops; and then watching each new wrinkle, the falling of each hair, the yellowing of teeth. I couldn't stand it. Don't tell me it is a misfortune to die young, in full gallop, not to wait like refuse in a dustbin for the scavenger to call. I'd rather put a bullet through my head."

A knock at the door. A pretty servant with a tray on which there was laid out what looked like afternoon tea.

"Put it down there," said Mr Robinson, pointing at a table, "and I ordered brandies. You can bring them straight up."

Miss Kelly, incapable of innovation, stared helplessly at the tray. They had finished dinner; tea was two meals away (whichever way you looked at it). What was it doing here? She was perturbed as by some sudden interruption in the natural order.

"I said *tea*," Mr Robinson explained.

"They took you at your word." Miss Kelly laughed. She had made a joke.

"I don't suppose we are compelled to eat it all." Mr Robinson took a survey: scones, sandwiches, sweet biscuits, fruit cake.

"I'm afraid that will put you back a small fortune," Miss Kelly said. The price of a thing was always uppermost in her mind. This prevented her from getting as much enjoyment as she might have out of her splendid income. The anachronistic

59

presence of the tea tray upset her. It looked "common", offended her sense of what was done; she would like to have put it out in the corridor, but that might have looked rude. From living in Australia, Mr Robinson had become inured to lodging-house habits. Any woman who married him would have to lead him gently back to how things should be.

"Tell me about Perth," she said. "What is life out there like? I simply can't imagine it."

"It's like any other modern city. I lived a good way out, in the country."

"And were there people of your own sort to meet? You had this taste for theatre for example. I can't imagine somehow . . ."

"I gave that up, cut it out completely. If you want to know how I spent my leisure time, I'll inform you. It isn't a secret, I used to practise remembering numbers, numbers of cars, telephone numbers, house numbers; that developed into keeping times in my mind, of ships, planes, trains. Once when I was thrown very much on my own company, I practised this. I collected timetables. When I had a place of my own, I bought maps; and I could tell at any time of the day or night what was happening almost anywhere. Now, for instance, it's half-past nine. We all know the Irish mail is leaving Euston. I could tell you what is happening in most of the principal railway stations. There's a plane bound for Amman leaving Orly in a quarter of an hour. Concorde will be—"

"I think that extraordinary—and fascinating," Miss Kelly interrupted fearing that Mr Robinson, if he got started, might be impossible to stop.

"And, tell me, if I am not being too inquisitive, where had you planned to retire to? Some of my friends have gone to the Isle of Man to get away from the taxes here, but things would have to become desperate before I'd do that. It is different, of course, for married people. They carry their home round on their back, Cyril says. Cyril—" She stopped. She had made a mistake. The chess board, the carpet slippers, the recital of hobbies—all Mr Robinson's efforts to show she had put his mind at rest had been dissipated by her loose tongue. She watched him undergo his Jekyll to Hyde transformation under

60

her eyes. As if she had threatened him, he subjected her to another of his appraising stares. She identified the expression: in nature, however long sustained, it would be followed by a pounce. What was she to do? Mentioning Cyril's name was the most natural thing in the world; he came into many of her conversations. It wasn't possible evidently to be oneself with Mr Robinson. Talking to him was like playing with a dangerous dog. But there was also something very childish about his behaviour. Why should she have to put up with it? Less than two days ago, she had never seen or heard of Mr Robinson, and she was not going to let him order her about. Cyril was one of her very oldest friends.

"Is anything the matter?"

She was encouraged by the calmness of her question.

"You said you wouldn't talk about me to Forbes. You promised—and there you go—"

"I don't understand you. You didn't ask me to suppress Cyril's name in our conversations. I promised not to talk about you to him. I don't think you had any right to ask me to. But I did. And I'm a person who keeps promises."

"You blether away, and most of the time you don't know what you are going to say next."

"I'm sorry if that is the impression you've formed of me. I didn't get the impression I was taking an undue share of our conversations. I don't feel like tackling that tea tray. It must weigh a ton. I'll ring downstairs and ask someone to remove it. I hope you won't think I'm being rude if I ask you to go now. I'm feeling rather tired and you have a journey before you."

She stood up and looked queenly. Mr Robinson, in carpet slippers, in a chair, was at a disadvantage. He might threaten, he might plead; she would not throw away her tactical advantage. In a play her hand would have been beside a bell. She didn't contemplate having to use a bell. If Mr Robinson rose to his feet, she would stare him down. Never since they met had she felt so in command. She wasn't intimidated by rudeness. That she recognised for what it was, and knew instinctively how to deal with it.

Mr Robinson did none of the things against which Miss Kelly

61

was so admirably armed. His face fell into his hands; he began to cry.

Miss Kelly had never seen a man crying before. Michael never cried. No man with whom she ever had anything to do had shown so much emotion. She didn't arouse it, had never experienced it. When she cried herself, it was from vexation, and because she was tired.

Mr Robinson was in extreme distress. She wasn't moved by it. She felt slightly embarrassed; but more like a householder when a pipe has burst than if any call were being made on her limited store of pity.

"Mr Robinson," she said, dropping her voice, "Please, Mr Robinson."

She abandoned her pose and sat down beside him waiting.

"Mr Robinson, let me give you some of your brandy."

She took the tumbler off the table where it flanked the enormous tray and, putting a hand on Mr Robinson's shoulder, raised the glass towards his face.

"Mr Robinson, try some of this."

He took his hands away from his face. He *had* been crying—she had half-suspected him of counterfeiting—and his tear-stained face looked pathetically young. He refused the brandy, but sat up, and she said, "That's right. That's better," as he, in her appropriate cliché, pulled himself together.

When she put the brandy in a place of safety, she turned to him again. His nerves, poor man, were in little pieces. The kindest thing she could do would be to persuade him to go to her doctor. She would talk to Mr Robinson in her wise and practical manner. It was long past the time for any nonsense, romantic or otherwise. Miss Kelly had come down to earth; it was, after all, the place where she was most at home.

"You must forgive me. I had no intention of being rude. You have been very kind to me, Miss Kelly. Once, when I was in a terrible situation, a woman was kind to me. I wasn't grateful at the time; I was young. Her goodness, the risk she ran—I accepted it as a tribute to my achievements and I was under the influence of the novel, that play—I can't separate them in my mind. You see I knew it would happen, that there would be this girl ready to face the future with me, a girl who knew everything, to whom I would confess all my secrets. So you see, when she turned up, I wasn't surprised or even grateful.

"It fell through. Her plan didn't work. She kept on writing to me, telling me she loved me. I had no time for that at all. I could see how it would be if I had been on her hands. I'd have had to spend most of my time—forgive me, Miss Kelly. But women are inclined to tie you to them with the ropes they provide for your escape."

"I don't understand. Explain. Please explain, Mr Robinson. I can't help you if you won't tell me what exactly it is that is upsetting you so much. Is it because you couldn't find your father's house? I'll go back there, if you like, and conduct a search on my own. I could take a photograph of it for you."

"My father has nothing to do with it. I hardly ever saw my father after I was thirteen. I was a nuisance and an embarrassment to him. And he refused to take me when my mother threw me out. I could sleep in the gutter so far as he was concerned. He told me that. But I never felt any hostility towards him. It was my mother who was in my way. So long as she was there I could never become anything. I was like some indoor plant in her house that she didn't even bother to water properly.

"My friend saw this. He said it was infamous that I should be held back by this perfectly useless creature. He had a very belittling way of talking about women, as if they were hardly human. He had postcards on the wall of his lavatory . . ."

"Mr *Robinson*!"

"I'm sorry. What does it matter? What are you made of Miss Kelly? Where does this pretence get you?

"But I didn't like it at the time. He was being so very nice to me and so concerned about me and making me feel important and admiring me—even my appearance. Nobody had ever . . . You see."

"Girls, girls. Surely, Mr Robinson, someone had told you, you were—"

"I hadn't anything to do with girls, Miss Kelly. I told you. I was always by myself."

"I think I'd rather . . ."

"What, Miss Kelly? What would you rather?"

"I'd as soon you didn't tell me too much . . . You know. One is always sorry for it afterwards."

"You've said something at last." Mr Robinson rose and waved his fists triumphantly.

"One is always sorry for it afterwards. How often have I found that out to my cost? Listen. My friend used to keep on about my mother. When I said her money would all be mine when she died, he told me I should demand my share now. He said it was my duty. Then came the day when my mother found the ten pound note gone after we had been alone in the house. I suspected my friend; I didn't like to admit it to myself, and I was not going to give my mother the ammunition to fire against him. I did as he told me. I told her I hadn't taken her money, but if I had, it was as much mine as hers. We had our first fight. No blows. Words. Before that I had let her nag and rage. It was easier than to get embroiled. But this time, I let her have it. I frightened her. She said she wouldn't let me sleep in the house any more. I could stay with my friend. Then she said she would make me an allowance.

"She didn't have to be frightened of me. I had no intention of harming her. I was not a violent person. Everything that hurt me went inside. And when I left her I was frightened of myself because I had frightened her. It was as if she had seen a me that wasn't myself. I was confused at the time because of the play. There's one place where the hero hears a man in a restaurant talking like my friend about the folly of letting a useless life stand in one's way. No great man would allow that to happen. I dreamed that I killed my mother, hit her on the head with an axe. Can you imagine it! But my life and my dreams were so confused then."

"What happened?"

"What *happened*, Miss Kelly?"

"Between you and your mother: did you go back to her?"

"She allowed me to come for meals. Often she was out, but she had a maid, a decent woman who cooked for us. She didn't mind if I invited my friend. She used not to tell. I always found out beforehand if my mother would be in or not. One day, when we were there, messing about—my friend used to like going over her possessions. She had some ivories—I saw him take a piece; he saw me, and put it back. On this particular day he told me I was a fool and that I should take whatever I liked. My mother would never have the nerve to prosecute me. When she died it would be mine anyway. I was only anticipating that joyful event.

"Did you say something just then Miss Kelly?"

"No, Mr Robinson, I didn't say a word."

"I didn't take anything, in case you thought I did. I wished that I could be strong enough to stand up to my mother and not have to depend on his support. Against her, I mean. I couldn't give up all that he was doing for me in other ways. I'd have preferred if he left my mother out of it; but he never let me forget her for a moment.

"This day, when I caught him trying to pinch the ivory, he became sour—he had never shown me that side of himself. He had been all sweetness to me; but his wasn't a sweet character. Vanity made me believe I knew the real person who wasn't known to the rest of the world. A man may have many sides, but he has only one centre. That doesn't change. I am the boy who swallowed too many sleeping-pills: you, Miss Kelly, are the little girl who peeped through the keyhole of your brother's dressing-room."

"Mr *Robinson*."

"Or something else. We can't fool one another, Miss Kelly, you and I. You may have lived in a glass case, but the same machinery ticks over under that expensive skirt of yours as under—".

"Mr Robinson. I think it's time—"

"I beg your pardon. No offence. But I must finish. My friend, as I was telling you when you interrupted me, got sour and pretended not to understand what I was trying to say, became elaborately polite—you know the method. I was afraid to offend, I depended so utterly on him. I was dominated by him completely. I would have done anything then to prevent his throwing me over. I was so little use to him, you see. He didn't need my help in his flat. He liked housework.

"Whatever got into him, he suggested that we should go into

my mother's bedroom and look at her clothes. She had locked it. Something new. Since the disappearance of the ten pound note, I suppose. Secretly, I was relieved. But my friend managed to open the lock. How could he do anything like that? Second nature. When we got in he walked around examining everything. Then he took the clothes out of her presses and drawers and laid them out on the bed. 'Put them on,' he said. And when I said there were too many, he said, 'Not all of them, silly donkey.' Not to waste time, I undressed. I did it to please him. It was all a rag, I thought; but I didn't like what I was doing, you understand. I was in my mother's silk underclothes and he was stark naked when she burst in. She screamed, screamed so loud that anyone passing on the road must have heard her. Then she left the room as suddenly as she came in."

"Why must you tell me these things, Mr Robinson? I don't want to hear them."

Miss Kelly's voice was very small because of the constriction in her throat. She felt damp and soiled and imprisoned, unable to escape, knowing she shouldn't be here or with him, would be happy and safe if only she could get away, and yet she was powerless to go. Some force kept her there waiting for more as if she were testing how far *she* could go, how much *she* could take.

"You brought up Cyril Forbes' name. I never mentioned him. I never give names, Miss Kelly. One name leads to another. I found that out long ago. When Forbes tells you about me, you must know the truth. I have been lied about. The most terrible lies, things you couldn't imagine, Miss Kelly, I have been accused of. Don't stare at me like that. Why are you staring at me, Miss Kelly? You are not afraid that I am going to, to—"

She shrieked, but there was very little sound when he stood up and looked down on her, his hands outspread. A look of hurt, like a rejected dog, came into his haunted eyes.

"What are you afraid of?"

"Nothing," Miss Kelly said. "It is only—" She was sobbing. "It is only that I'm not used to hearing . . . I'm upset. It's all right. It was silly of me."

He looked at her fondly, stretched out a hand. At the zoo, as a child, she had been told not to accept overtures made from behind cage bars. Hesitantly, her hand met Mr Robinson's. A warm strong male hand. The relief was overwhelming. She grasped it. Mr Robinson was on his knees, his face in her chest. She stroked his head very gently. No longer afraid.

"There," she said. "You mustn't worry. I won't tell Cyril. I promise."

Mr Robinson's arms now encircled her, but for comfort. He looked up.

"What is it?" she enquired.

He seemed to be making sure of her identity, noting from whom the kindness came.

"Are you comfortable?

Mr Robinson looked awkward on his knees. Miss Kelly's practical sense, in the ascendant again, assured her he would be more comfortable in a chair. At that he got up. She had a moment of panic. He was so touchy; had she started him off again? But Mr Robinson did not look offended. "Excuse me. I'll be back in a moment," he said, backing out of the room. "It's the third door on the left," Miss Kelly called after him. Grateful for the interruption, she took a quick look at her face in the mirror, and then moved to the dressing-table. She would have liked above everything a long, cleansing bath.

When Mr Robinson returned, her face had been powdered, her hair patted into place. He had evidently come to a resolution of some sort. His manner was of the foreman of a jury returning with the verdict. There was no trace of the sick animal that Miss Kelly had petted, but she recognised what she had come to call the "Enoch look" in his eye: a god of wrath, biding his time.

He refused to sit down. He must be getting to bed. He would see her in the morning. She was disappointed, and still she knew that this was right. Like some books in which she had seen shocking things and went on reading them, with one side of herself ashamed, but curiosity the stronger when it came to the tug o' war, Mr Robinson's revelations were better put out of reach. She would have liked to hear even ever so little more. And yet it was better not. How often had she comforted herself: "I don't suppose anything ever happened really."

Now he was gone, and she was safe, and all was well. Tomorrow he might have time for a stroll along the cliff walk, where she had seen him on his first morning. Already it seemed that she had known Mr Robinson for years. He had terrified her; she couldn't go through *that* again. Less than an hour ago, she would have blessed anyone who removed Mr Robinson from her sight and guaranteed that he would never return; and now she wondered how she could stay in this place, surrounded by people she didn't know, waiting for Cyril. After Mr Robinson, Cyril would be so . . . so old-maidish.

Whatever was odd about him—and everything about Mr Robinson except his clothes was odd—there was no doubt about his masculinity. That should have made the business about dressing-up in his mother's clothes seem harmless; but it had given her an impression of evil. The other man—the one he called his friend—was the villain. To talk like that to anyone about his mother, however inadequate she might be—unbelievable! It was all exaggerated, of course; but Miss Kelly couldn't get out of her mind what Mr Robinson's mother saw when she came into her room, her son in her underclothes and this other person, this friend—the word as Mr Robinson used it had taken on a nasty sinister sound—this friend, lying on the bed, naked. Was he going to dress up too? Was that all it meant? But to come into one's bedroom and find——And where did Cyril come into all this? She could imagine Cyril's giggling if she told the story in a certain way; but there was nothing—she searched for the word—"unwholesome" about Cyril. He was always the same, like herself in a way, gradually getting older; nothing had ever happened to them, they had ceased to be children; that was all. Of one thing she was certain, whatever Mr Robinson had to fear, nobody would be more alarmed than Cyril if he were to hear that Mr Robinson's friend had been described as a friend of his. To imagine that jeering, *naked* man at one of Cyril's parties, with Mrs Cantwell, Lady Jamieson, Arthur Aldwell, and Mrs Knox Knox—the idea was frankly absurd, but too uncomfortable to be the subject of laughter.

All things considered, Miss Kelly was not going to tell anyone about Mr Robinson. He was better in every way kept as a secret.

She would get his address and give him hers and they could write to each other. But he was not likely to write very good letters. They would be very noncommittal, she felt sure. Like her own. Some people could make up so much about nothing; but she found when she was writing to someone, except to begin "My dear", instead of simply, "Dear", and to alter the words at the end a little, she would never do more than put down things she had done recently; and they never seemed to amount to much more than one might have known without being told. She took trouble over her stationery, of course, and wrote a clear, round hand. Cyril's handwriting was marvellous, like a drunken spider's.

Miss Kelly went to sleep at last, excited about the morning. She had a nightmare. She was in the House of Commons. Enoch Powell was making a speech about black people. Miss Kelly began to applaud him loudly. Then she discovered that she was being looked at by everyone. She was interrupting the speech. Mr Powell was staring at her. Instead of being grateful for her support, he obviously regarded her clapping and cheers as an interruption. She didn't know what to do. Then she looked down and saw that she had nothing on. Not a stitch. She was lying in a grass hollow at Bunbeg. Mr Robinson was staring at her; he looked very terrible. "I thought I was in my bath," she tried to explain. He pointed down to the sands at the foot of Slieve League. He was insisting she should look. She felt ashamed, being in her skin, but she came beside him and looked down. She saw herself, down below, lying in the foam on the shingle beneath the cliff. The little murmuring waves crept up the naked body, and very gently crawled over it. "I must put on my clothes. Where are my clothes?" she was crying. The gulls flew round, mocking her. Mr Robinson didn't seem to hear her, and didn't seem to care. She was here, miles away from everywhere, in broad daylight with not a stitch to put on. He was cruel.

It was six o'clock when she woke. She tried to sleep again, tried to read. The time crept by. She could hear sounds of life, voices outside, rattles of buckets, revving of motors. Milk deliveries, she supposed. Feet moved on the floor overhead. She couldn't appear downstairs before eight. She decided to take a bath.

Lazing in the bath, she thought about her dream. Not that she would ever dare to tell Mr Robinson about it. He had said that when he was so obsessed with the play he was acting in—or *was* he acting in it?—she couldn't remember—he became so confused between the story and his own life and his dreams and reality, he couldn't distinguish between them. It looked as if he might be having the same effect on her. Mr Robinson had certainly made life more interesting. Almost too interesting. It was, perhaps, as well that he was going away.

She came down to breakfast at eight o'clock precisely. The French fisherfolk were already in the dining-room. Mr Robinson's table was unoccupied. In twos and threes the other residents filed in. By half-past eight most of the tables were occupied. Of Mr Robinson still no sign.

At nine o'clock, Miss Kelly left her table. Ashamed and astonished at herself, she asked the proprietor's wife, who happened to be standing in the hall, had she seen Mr Robinson.

"Oh, he left this morning. He had to catch a very early train."

Part 2

I

CYRIL'S VISIT WAS not a success. To begin with, his train was late; he strained his back—he said—carrying his case out to the car at the station. His back dominated the holiday; its behaviour was capricious in the extreme and hovered over the social engagements Miss Kelly had made round the county. It was uncertain each day whether Cyril would be fit to venture out. Other excursions could not be considered in any event. The weather deteriorated from the moment he arrived, and picked up again on the morning he set out with Miss Kelly for Dublin.

A poltergeist was at work from the start; wherever they went, when the spirits of the party were not depressed by the topic of Cyril's back, some guest fell out at the last moment, or someone arrived uninvited and overtaxed the table, or a husband and wife let their domestic disagreements sabotage the evening. Miss Kelly was glad to say goodbye to Donegal.

Anger at Mr Robinson's disappearance cauterised the wound to her self-regard: rudeness, bad manners—these she would not tolerate. More subtle injuries she might not always recognise; but she knew how people she admitted to her friendship should behave; and this was gross. It cancelled out any undertakings she gave him under the pretext of friendship. Fortunately, she had left nothing of herself in the custody of his chivalry. The man had none. Absent, it was impossible to explain, even to herself, how a creature so eccentric could have exercised such a power of fascination. So far from being tempted to speak about him to Cyril—or to anyone—she felt guilty and ashamed: she had let herself down, lowered her standards. The things she had let him say to her! But he had *done* nothing. She would come out successfully from the severest cross-examination. That was a comforting thought, not that she would ever have to undergo any such experience on Mr Robinson's account.

"How's the cough?" Cyril had said on arrival. For a moment she hadn't caught his drift. So fully occupied had she been, she simply forgot the reason for coming to Donegal had been a cold, and not to meet Mr Robinson.

When alone with Cyril she sometimes found herself asking questions without premeditation, and under some compulsion. Because they never sounded spontaneous—with his back injuries, Cyril had enough to put up with—he was sometimes short with his replies. He couldn't believe her sudden interest in Australia and Australians was genuine, for example, and replied to her question that he had never been in Australia and had heard that it was like Canada, only worse, or perhaps it was that Canada was like Australia, only worse; he couldn't remember. He had found difficulty in concealing his impatience when she got sulky when he refused to hurry to see Enoch Powell on television, and afterwards went on about him so. Miss Kelly pretending to artistic interests was even more trying, because patently insincere—cross-questioning him about theatres, for example. What was the name of the novel that had been turned into a play and acted at the Phoenix Theatre? She was vague about its plot, an old woman gets killed with an axe. The hero gives the blow to free himself from inhibitions. Cyril didn't try to remember; but later that evening said: "You were thinking of *Crime and Punishment*."

"Who is that by? Don't tell me. I know. Chekhov. I saw *The Cherry Orchard*." She smiled complacently.

Cyril couldn't be bothered to correct her. Really, she was becoming too tiresome. Could it be "the change"? It must be about due; and it took women in different ways. He would be better able to bear Miss Kelly when his back was itself again.

Cyril had to be driven across Dublin to Killiney, adding forty miles to Miss Kelly's return journey. She was tired when she arrived home, and glad to be there. Never could she remember the view across the estuary look so superb as this evening. The clouds had banked down over the setting sun concentrating the red glow on the water. It seemed to burn.

She loved her own house. It looked welcoming. Mrs Ridley was at the door when she pulled up; Mr Ridley came out to fetch her luggage. Her retriever, Lupin, came rushing out; he almost knocked her over. It was worth going away for such a return. Indoors everything was as it should be; a fire was alight in the library, the room she used when she was not entertaining. In her bedroom, the bedclothes were turned down, her nightdress laid out. Mrs Ridley produced tea, hot scones and honey within ten minutes of her arrival. What calls had there been, she enquired, and was informed. All of no consequence. She looked at her letters. Nothing to annoy. This was the ceiling of her entertainment; after came a series of reductions. They began with the information that Mrs Ridley's brother who lived—needless to say—in the country, was dangerously ill. She had held off the pressures to go at once to see him until Miss Kelly's safe return, but she couldn't refuse the call. She must, with Miss Kelly's sanction, go to the remotest part of Clare tomorrow, and Mr Ridley must go with her.

Miss Kelly agreed to this, and even expressed regret for the condition of Mrs Ridley's brother; but it required an effort, and did not—nor was intended to—produce a glow. The working class, Miss Kelly had all her life observed, made the illness of relatives an excuse for withdrawing their labour. In her own class, illness made only such claims on one's time as it took to pay a visit to a nursing home or order a sheaf of flowers from the florist. Mrs Ridley would be away next day, that night and, if her brother (which God forbid) were to get worse or die, she might be away for some days. She would leave as much as possible prepared. Mrs Donnelly, up the road, had promised to come and assist; but she wouldn't be available until Wednesday. That meant Miss Kelly would have no help tomorrow.

"I'll ring Aggie up," Miss Kelly said to herself. And when she did, Aggie was sympathy itself, but she was going to help at a nephew's party and couldn't disappoint the child. That meant Miss Kelly must dine alone tomorrow; but Aggie would be down soon after dinner, having eaten birthday fare. How typical of Aggie! She was too prone to commit herself, to be made use of. It was from weakness as much as good-nature, wanting to be all things to all women since Joe Fitzsimons left her a widow in Dublin where widows are expected to commit the social

equivalent of suttee. When Miss Kelly first took her up she had
been utterly reliable and prepared to cancel at short notice any
engagement to suit her friend's convenience; but her sense of
obligation had noticeably weakened of late. She tried to "fit in"
conflicting calls. It was tiresome.

Mrs Ridley got breakfast on Tuesday morning, laid out a cold
lunch and put a dinner in the oven. "You have only to switch it
on at six o'clock," she explained, trying to minimise the incon-
venience she was causing. Miss Kelly's muted tone dampened
any prospect of that. Strictly, Miss Kelly was not alone, she had
Donnelly who worked all day on the place, and lived in a cottage
less than a hundred yards from her gate. What she chiefly
resented was to be reminded that paying staff did not give you an
absolute claim on their services.

She had no trouble employing herself; arranging flowers—the
dahlias were better than ever—and she worked at *petit point* in
competition with Cyril. She had never examined the library
assembled by her father, to which Michael had added about a
thousand volumes. An idea occurred to her when she was working at her embroidery. Could *Crime and Punishment* be, by any
chance, among the books in the house? Michael's taste did not
lie in the direction of Russian novels, but his father had taken
advice when he made his collection, and Chekhov was a name
that might well have been on his list. Because it was so seldom
resorted to—visitors occasionally took a book down—the library
was in good order, and Miss Kelly soon discovered that there
was a plan. Ancient books in leather bindings that nobody could
ever possibly want to read were massed together at eye level.
These she could ignore. There were most of the English novel-
ists she had heard of. Shakespeare and other poets. Balzac in an
English translation. One volume of Chekhov's short stories, but
nothing else. There were Tolstoy's novels and Turgenev's
and—her Guardian Angel must have put it there—*Crime and
Punishment*. By Dostoevsky, though. She took out the book,
settled herself on the carpet, and browsed through it to see if
there was some explanation. Gradually, it dawned upon her that
she must have made a mistake. Surprisingly, though, Cyril who
rather prided himself on being well-read hadn't known.

The novel was quite easy to read, but as she proceeded she felt a growing hostility to the seediness of the story's setting and the unpronounceability of the characters' names. She was irritated as some people are in a foreign country when they ask a question in the language and are not understood. They raise their voices. They are driven mad by the low level of intelligence that cannot hear a simple question emphatically spoken. As if the names were not difficult enough, they were changed sometimes without warning. By judicious skipping she had mastered the plot by dinner time, but it gave her no help at all in explaining Mr Robinson. The hero, an impossible young man, killed an old woman pawnbroker and her sister, who had arrived on the scene at the inappropriate moment. After that the book seemed to consist of interminable conversations. She read carefully the chapter in which Raskolnikov confesses to Sonia, the angelic prostitute; Mr Robinson had said, Miss Kelly remembered, that his attention had been riveted by this scene when he was watching rehearsals. She read the part near the end where the student is sent to Siberia and Sonia goes with him.

He had got off pretty lightly; and the girl's carry-on seemed far-fetched and ridiculous. Even if she had become a prostitute because there was no other way of getting money—and Miss Kelly accepted this as understandable if deplorable—it was inexplicable that any decent girl would not be revolted by a man who had killed two women with an axe. The idea was utterly repellent. Even if it were in self-defence, Miss Kelly was sure that she could never allow the hand that had performed such an act to touch her. And as to . . . She put the book back. It had been a dreary anti-climax, as—when she came to think of it—everything connected with Mr Robinson had been. He had startled and alarmed and hypnotised her; on a few occasions she felt sure that he was going to overcome the scruples of a lifetime, but always there had been a change of mood, a postponement. Finally, he had absconded, like a lodger in arrears with his rent. She shook her head to get him out of it. He made her feel slightly doped and ashamed of herself, as if she had been too self-indulgent; if this went on, she would feel the need to mention it in confession. But how? She had such a miserable list of sins to tell as a rule, going to confession was a routine like going to the dentist when her teeth were still as sound and white as when he first inspected them. How would she categorise her obsession? "I have had impure thoughts, Father." But *had* she? Was that a fair description of the state of her mind? "I thought he was going to make advances to me and I had not quite decided, if he did, whether to do anything to prevent him." Was that the truth? How did she know, until the moment arrived, what she might have done? Thinking too much about Mr Robinson was a form of self-indulgence, but if not about him, it would have been about something, possibly, quite futile. She never pretended to great thoughts, but tried only to do what she thought right.

It was so comfortable in the kitchen that she ate her meal there, quite enjoying the informality. On an impulse, she went back to the library, coffee cup in hand. There was something she remembered about Mr Robinson's *friend* that she wanted to check. Where did *he* come in? There was this character, absurdly called Razoumikhin, but he seemed to be amiable, certainly not a bad influence. The examining magistrate—there was a great deal about him; but it was incessant discussion, mostly with Raskolnikoff (what a *ridiculous* name!) and designed, it seemed, to fix guilt for the crime on him.

She couldn't take seriously all that stuff about Napoleon, how committing a crime, even murder, could liberate a man's spirit and make him capable of anything. The magistrate, whatever *his* name was, had read these ideas apparently in some article the student had written, and was suggesting that they were inconvenient views for someone who was under suspicion for a crime—a confession in advance, as it were.

Mr Robinson had said that the effect of all this on him was to make him lose his own sense of sequence in time. Here was one example of what might have confused him. The book was so crazy in every respect. Such dotty people, and in a state bordering on hysteria in any circumstances. But it would be interesting to discover where Mr Robinson's friend, to whom he was so careful not to give a name, came in. Mr Robinson was uncanny in this respect. He must have some horror of proper names. She found the book and began to flip through it, sitting again on her thick carpet, sipping her coffee, interested at first, but her attention began to wander during a long scene in a pub near the beginning. Someone with the most ridiculous name of all—Marmeladoff—talked away in that, a drunken, elderly, good-for-nothing. That could not be Mr Robinson's friend. She came across a conversation between a student and a young officer, quite early on in the story. They are talking about the old pawnbroker woman everyone dislikes so much, and her sister, who is over-sized and, in spite of that, always getting pregnant. Feeble-minded almost certainly. (Miss Kelly was on the committee of a home for unmarried mothers, run by nuns, and she had heard that feeble-mindedness led to illegitimate children.) The student is all in favour of killing the pawnbroker. "A hundred, a thousand good deeds and enterprises could be carried out and upheld with the money this old woman had bequeathed to a monastery. A dozen families might be saved from hunger, want, ruin, crime and misery, and all with her money."

Miss Kelly closed the book. It was too silly, terribly Russian. Then she opened it again to see if Raskolnikov went to bed with the saintly prostitute at the end of the confession scene. It was a detail; but as she would not read the book again she might as well know.

She had not found the place when she heard the welcome sound of car wheels on the gravel outside, and Aggie's confident push on the door-bell. Before she had crossed the hall to meet the widow, her irritation with Aggie had disappeared. She was really a dear, rushing away from her nephew's birthday party because her friend was alone. An hour's drive too. So Miss Kelly put on her most welcoming smile behind the door before she threw it open. She was met by reflections of light from the hall on the gravel, dark shadows in the middle-distance under a blue-black sky, packed with stars. But nobody was there. She was shutting the door when a figure came out from behind one of the pillars of the porch. Mr Robinson stood in the doorway.

II

"YOU GAVE ME such a fright," Miss Kelly said when she got her breath back, "I was expecting somebody else." Mr Robinson stepped over the threshold with the manner of a man who had called to retrieve yesterday's hat. Indoors he turned to Miss Kelly.

"As I was in the neighbourhood, I thought I should call to apologise for my rather hasty departure in Donegal. I was going to write to you. When I get an impulse, I tend to act upon it, and I wanted to get away from that place before your friend arrived."

"But he couldn't travel by train from Dublin to Donegal and arrive before breakfast."

"Very true, but when you sleep as badly as I do, the night is so long you think the day begins long before you come down to breakfast. I had my bag packed since the night before. I was restless. I had to be on the move."

"You could have rung my room or even left a note. I must say, I thought you behaved very uncivilly."

"If I spoke to you on the telephone, you might have persuaded me to delay. I was afraid of that. The sort of man I am, Miss Kelly, when I have something on my mind, I put everything else aside and do it."

"Everything else included me on this occasion."

"I intended to write."

"You didn't."

"I knew we would be meeting again."

"And how, pray, did you know that? But we have been standing long enough. I was sitting in here when the bell rang."

She led the way into the library, where her coffee cup lay on the carpet beside her book. She saw them, and bent down to pick them up off the floor.

"Allow me," said Mr Robinson.

Their heads nearly collided. Miss Kelly got her hand on the cup and saucer, Mr Robinson picked up the book. She saw him reading the title. She panicked. "I'll put that away." She almost snatched it out of his hand. When she had replaced it on the shelf she went straight across the room and put a match to the fire.

"A room in the evening without a fire is depressing, I always think, even with central heating."

As Mr Robinson made no comment, she continued to tend the fire, making her cheeks red in the process.

"There, I think that will do. I thought you were Mrs Fitz-simons, a friend of mine who is staying with me, when I heard you ring at the door. May I get you something to drink? Have you had your dinner?"

She had not looked at Mr Robinson until now. He hadn't moved from where he had picked up the book. He might have been doing a complicated sum in his head, judging by his expression. In his own time he joined Miss Kelly, standing with his back to the fireplace.

"I see you have been reading *Crime and Punishment*."

"Not really. I was browsing through the shelves just before you arrived, looking for something to read. I'm not much of a reader, and I must try to read more, I'm so much alone and we really have quite a fine collection of books."

"I wonder why you picked on that particular volume." Mr Robinson let his wild eyes travel around the thousands of books on display and travel back and down to where Miss Kelly, curled up on the sofa, had been sitting when he arrived.

"I've never read it before. It's a very famous book. But it looks rather long and rambling. I couldn't get through *Anna Karenina*. And I wanted to read that after seeing it on television. I saw the film once; but I can't remember it very well. It was so long ago."

She was running on from embarrassment; Mr Robinson, she knew, although she didn't dare to peep, was looking at her out of the corner of his eye.

"But why, I wonder, did you suddenly get this inspiration?"

"You know how it is: the name of a book flashes into your

81

mind or you hear it mentioned and you decide you must read it. Surely that often happens to you?"

"What interests me is, why this particular book? I don't think it's in the news at present. Where did you hear it mentioned?"

"Nowhere in particular. I came in and looked and it happened to be on the first shelf I examined. You see so many of the books are not books anyone could possibly read. I don't suppose they've been taken down since Father put them up there more than twenty years before I was born. He was nearly sixty when he married my mother, you know."

"To come back to my question: did anyone mention that particular book in your hearing recently? I'm interested to know."

"I don't think so."

"Cyril Forbes wasn't talking about it by any chance?"

"He may have been—oh yes, now that you mention it, I remember his saying something about it: but I don't think he can ever have read it because he thinks it was written by Chekhov."

"What makes you say that?"

"He didn't actually say so, but I did. I'm not really a booky person, you know. He didn't contradict me, and he is for ever contradicting me as a rule. This time his back was giving him such trouble, he wasn't really in form for anything. I'm just as glad you didn't stay. The weather was terrible, and there seemed to be a jinx on his holiday."

"What I'd be interested to hear is how you brought up the subject of a book of which you didn't know the name of the author. What put it in your mind in the first place?"

"I just can't remember. I told you. It doesn't matter. It's not worth discussing."

"But it is. It interests me enormously. You manage somehow to discuss a book that you have never read, and whose author you don't know the name of, with someone who doesn't know the name of the author either. How did the discussion arise in the first place? That is what interests me."

"I can't remember. Cyril talks a great deal, and I chat away, chiefly to pass the time—Cyril, as a rule is the most cheerful company. That is when he's feeling well. We never go into things deeply. He's not that sort of person. It suits me. I can't keep up with brainy people. I find them boring as a rule. I know there are exceptions. I met the Archbishop at dinner recently. He was quite a pet. We talked about the times when we had arrived late at parties or forgot to go. It was great fun."

"You didn't mention my name to Forbes by any chance?"

"Of course not. I promised you I wouldn't, didn't I? I never even said you were there. Cyril must have thought I had a very dull time before he came."

"Did you mention my friend?"

"What friend?"

"You know. I only talked to you about one."

"How could I? I didn't even know his name. You never told me."

"You managed to discuss a book that you didn't know the name of."

"I didn't say that. I said I thought it was by Chekhov. It was a very easy mistake to make."

"Did Cyril Forbes tell you about the plot of the novel?"

"No. He didn't talk about it at all."

"I thought you said you discussed it with him."

"It was mentioned in passing. You know how it is. I don't know why you are making such an issue of it. May I get you something to drink?"

"In a moment. Did you bring up the subject of the Phoenix Theatre, by any chance?"

"I don't think so. It might have been mentioned casually when we were discussing Chekhov. Cyril takes me to the theatre sometimes. And we quite often go together to the Wexford Opera Festival. That is something you might really enjoy. Will you be in this country in October, by any chance? I might be able . . ."

"Were you going to suggest I should make a trio with Cyril Forbes? Miss Kelly, I don't think you are to be trusted."

"Mr Robinson!"

He had taken her hands.

"Look at me. Tell me what you said to Cyril Forbes about me."

The door-bell rang. Aggie Fitzsimons felt doubly rewarded for her effort to escape from the party. Never had Miss Kelly—who was so generous about giving presents, but so exacting—never had she been so loving and welcoming.

"Aggie, dear, how kind, kind, kind you were to come. Aggie, this is Mr Robinson, a friend of mine from Australia. Mrs Fitzsimons left a party early to keep me company."

"You didn't need me after all," Aggie said.

"Mr Robinson only dropped in. A surprise. I didn't expect him. We were waiting for you before we had a drink. What shall it be?"

"I'm very full of lemonade. I think I'd like whiskey. Only a little drop."

"And you, Mr Robinson?"

"I must be on my way."

"You'll make me feel I drove you out," Mrs Fitzsimons said.

"Do have something before you go. It seems so inhospitable . . ." Miss Kelly put on a wheedling expression. Mr Robinson was obdurate. The widow was left sitting at the fire, but the door of the library was not closed by Miss Kelly when she saw Mr Robinson out.

"Are you staying somewhere? You wouldn't like a bed for the night?"

"I'm staying at the hotel in Malahide. I'll arrange an evening, when your friend goes home. You might dine with me."

"That would be very nice," Miss Kelly said, but she felt no kindness towards Mr Robinson. She didn't want to see him again. He had been definitely unpleasant. Interrogating her like a detective. What nerve! Why had she not flatly refused to be cross-examined like that, in her own house, by a man she knew nothing about, an almost total stranger? It was ridiculous. But he had caught her off-guard. The book on the floor was unfortunate; and she had lost her head completely when he began to question her. She should never have admitted to anything. He was convinced that she had spoken to Cyril. How could she get out of another interview without being rude? She would tell

84

Aggie. She had to confide in someone. Lucky she came then. The blessing of God!

Aggie listened, fascinated by her proud friend's narrative. At times she was stupid, and had to ask her for certain incidents to be explained, and Miss Kelly's explanation of the plot of *Crime and Punishment* was double Dutch to Mrs Fitzsimons. She drew her own conclusions before Miss Kelly had made an end. This was a roundabout way of confessing to a romance in the manner of the novels of Ethel M. Dell, that she had been forbidden to read as a child: they were the only reading of her nurse, who had bought them in a bundle at a jumble sale for a shilling.

Mr Robinson had the appearance of a strong, silent man, who might, under provocation, produce a horsewhip. He looked very like somebody Aggie thought she knew. For her taste, he was too intimidating to be likeable. But she could see how Miss Kelly might be susceptible to someone more arrogant even than herself. Miss Kelly, telling the story, found herself cutting it, not to save time—she had all night and the next day—but in the narration she was sometimes embarrassed by her matter. It made her guilty by association. She would appear to have encouraged Mr Robinson to indulge in pornographic reminiscence. For instance, she garbled out of recognition that scene in Mrs Robinson's bedroom, leaving her audience under the impression that she wasn't hearing the whole story—which indeed was the case—and believing that what was being kept back from her was the part Miss Kelly had played. Mrs Fitzsimons could not visualise her friend sitting all that time listening merely to anyone's endless narrative about his childhood and youth. She was waiting for a confession or, at least, a request for advice as to what Miss Kelly should do in her infatuated state. Because she had put this construction on Miss Kelly's confidence and had the evidence of her own eyes that Mr Robinson was not a fiction, she was too busy divining Miss Kelly's secret to listen carefully to her story.

"What do you make of it at all?" Miss Kelly enquired, catching her friend unawares. She did her best, improvising.

"I think you ought to know him better before you get yourself too deeply involved. I don't know if I ever told you, but before I

85

was engaged to Fergus, I met this very attractive mining engineer who had come with a Canadian company to explore for minerals in County Cork. My experience was so like yours, that when you were telling me, I almost felt I was there. This engineer--Harold Winterbloom was his name—I think he was partly Jewish, not that I would have minded that particularly. . . ."

Miss Kelly, not listening, wondered why Aggie didn't leave her hair alone, and stopped her in mid-sentence to say that she had an idea. She would ring up Mr Robinson at the hotel in Malahide in the morning and invite him to dinner. If he accepted, Aggie would be there for one, and someone else could be roped in. ("Father Barry always comes when I invite him.") Then she would have done the right thing, and she could firmly refuse any invitation coming from him.

Aggie, thrown at full gallop, agreed. This visit promised to be more exciting than life was usually at Miss Kelly's. Afterwards, they talked; Miss Kelly made chocolate. Sometimes she reverted to the subject of Mr Robinson, and when she had finished, Mrs Fitzsimons brought up the irrelevant and uninteresting topic of the mining engineer, whose existence, Miss Kelly considered, was largely invention.

They went to bed.

"I don't suppose it would be too early to ring up Mr Robinson now," Miss Kelly said to her friend next morning. They had finished breakfast.

Mrs Fitzsimons approved. "You may catch him before he goes out." She heard Miss Kelly on the telephone. "But when did he leave?"

Over her shoulder, to her friend, Miss Kelly exclaimed, "He's gone." Then, into the telephone, "Thank you very much. Did he leave a forwarding address? Oh, well, it doesn't matter. Thank you."

"This is the Donegal story all over again," Miss Kelly said when she had seated herself. "It's so rude. I don't mind anything else; I won't put up with rudeness."

"I'm sure there is some explanation. He will call you during the day. But, frankly, dear, are you not well rid of him? He doesn't seem to me to be any social asset. His behaviour is so odd, I'd be afraid . . ."

"What would *you* be afraid of?"

"That he might do something really upsetting. You don't know him long, do you? It's always wise to be cautious about people you meet in hotels on holiday. They fit in at the time, but if they look you up in your own surroundings, they never seem to fit; and they've lost their glamour somehow. I remember after I met this mining engineer I was telling you about—"

"Aggie, what did you mean when you said just now *something really upsetting*?"

As Aggie hadn't any clear idea in her mind, she had to improvise again.

"Be rude to one of your guests or become unpleasant in some other way. He might be utterly unsociable. That wouldn't suit you, my dear."

"To hear you, Aggie, one would imagine I was seriously considering Mr Robinson as a beau. I am past the age for beaux; and if Mr Robinson has kept out of women's clutches until his present age, he's unlikely to be thinking of changing his ways now."

Miss Kelly had forgotten how grateful she was for Aggie's timely arrival last night; now, she saw her friend as an intruder. What was Mr Robinson going to say or do when he grasped her hands? Like steel his were. They had hurt her; but it was thrilling as well as frightening. No man had ever hurt her before; there was a girl at school, when she was little, who used to pinch the younger ones in chapel. That was different. She would have liked to talk about Mr Robinson, to analyse his behaviour and see what conclusions might be drawn from what he had seemed so urgent to tell about himself. But she was inhibited; she saw the banal construction Aggie was putting on the whole affair, and her patience had been worn thin— whenever Mr Robinson was mentioned—by the inevitable retaliatory reminiscence about the wretched mining engineer. When Aggie said she had to run up to town in the afternoon, Miss Kelly didn't offer to go with her.

Mrs Ridley rang up from Bantry to say her brother was approaching his end. Miss Kelly agreed that this, if it had to come, couldn't come too soon. That meant at least two more days for funeral and attendant rites on top of the dying time, whatever that might be.

"Would you like to come out to dinner? There's quite a good restaurant in Malahide," Miss Kelly offered, but Mrs Fitzsimons declared that a needless extravagance. She would be perfectly content with an omelette, and no one knew better how to make one. Talking her head off, she left for Dublin at two-thirty.

Miss Kelly was glad enough of the respite. She preferred her own company today; Aggie's insistence on her right to romantic reminiscence made her an inadequate confidante. Mr Robinson's most recent misdemeanour, while it convinced her that he was not a social asset, an unlikely friend, and an impossible husband, made him an even more intriguing subject for contemplation. Aggie had divined something unstable about him—he *had* been frightening when he seized her hands—but how drab he made the daily round, how mediocre and repetitive her friends!

"Oh, is that *you*?" she had caught herself saying to them on the telephone, inviting "Who did you think it might be?"— giving herself away, like a schoolgirl with a crush.

After half an hour of stern self-denial, she rang up the Grand Hotel again and enquired had Mr Robinson returned. He had not. Was he expected? He was not. The receptionist was polite and impersonal; there was no reason for Miss Kelly to flush from self-consciousness. The library, since last night, was too charged with Mr Robinson's psyche even for her to enter it. She worked ineffectually in the garden for an hour, and then went down the road to call on Mrs Donnelly to make sure she was available during the weekend if the Ridleys had not come back by then. It was an unnecessary journey, Donnelly had already vouched for his wife, but it was something to do, and when Miss Kelly was agitated, as she was today, Mrs Donnelly was an effective emollient.

She apologised for the trouble Miss Kelly had put herself to

("Didn't Tod tell you I was coming, straight after breakfast?"), then she lamented "the terrible times that was in it" and averred that "not a day passed but she thanked God Mr Michael *wasn't in it*. There's no place any longer for a gentleman the likes of him."

Miss Kelly was grateful for the nostalgic reminder of better days (Michael had been chronically out of sorts), and yet again came away without registering her complaint that Mrs Donnelly, having recently raised her charges, left invariably on one pretext or another half an hour before her stipulated time.

She had killed a substantial part of the afternoon; now she would make herself a cup of tea and begin preparations for some sort of supper for Aggie. Really, she would have been better on her own; why had she called on Aggie so impulsively when Mrs Ridley announced her desertion? She didn't mind being alone, was used to it in fact. The Donnellys were almost within call if she needed any assistance; there were always little things going wrong and she couldn't turn a screw or hammer in a nail. She rather prided herself on her soft hands and her useless fingers.

The Donnellys' cottage was on the main road; a short distance further along the road a lane led down to the estuary shore. Between stone walls, it was sometimes used for parking caravans by what Miss Kelly still described as "tinkers". She had been agitating for action against these undesirables for years, and any sign of their presence agitated her considerably. She was convinced that they came here with the express purpose of robbing her.

In the distance—she wasn't wearing her spectacles—she saw a man behaving in a peculiar fashion. He seemed to be measuring the width of the lane. He had disappeared when she arrived at the spot and found, to her relief, no sign of caravans. She could prolong her walk by keeping along the shore of the estuary by the path and striking back where it ended in a cul de sac. Once again the weather was mocking her holiday. The water reflected the plangent blue of the sky and, out at sea, Malahide Island looked so near that if she stretched out a hand she could touch it. An infallible sign of rain but, for the moment, enchanting.

The man who had been measuring the road was surveying the scene through field-glasses. Miss Kelly almost collided with him, coming round a bend, not looking where she was going, all eyes on the view. She apologised and broke off, startled when she recognised Mr Robinson.

"Oh, it's you," she said. "What do you think of the view?"

"Has your friend gone home?" he replied, proof against Miss Kelly's conversational gambits.

"She had to go up to Dublin this afternoon. She is staying with me very kindly until Mrs Ridley comes back."

"This place hasn't changed."

"You remember it?"

"Yes, Miss Kelly, I remember it."

"I saw you measuring the lane just now." As soon as she had spoken the words she knew she would regret it.

"What did you say?"

"I thought I saw you measuring the lane; but I may have been imagining it."

"I don't know what you are talking about."

"I must have imagined it, anyhow it can't have been you. Where's your car?"

"I left it on the road. I wanted to see this part, where the land ends. It looks as if people come here. It used to be quite deserted."

"There were always loving couples in their cars in the evening. I remember when I was young walking my dog along and pretending not to be aware."

"How long ago would that have been, Miss Kelly?"

"When I was a teenager."

"I put the question rather tactlessly, I'm afraid. I was only interested to know how far back your memory of the spot is. Do you remember it so long ago as the last war for instance?"

"I'm afraid I do, and even before that."

"Forgive my question."

"You are being very polite."

"Am I not always?"

"I'm afraid not, not when you rush away from hotels before breakfast without leaving messages."

"Were you looking for me in Malahide?"

"I was, to invite you to dinner, but I might have known you would light out before the milk arrived."

"I didn't say I was going to stay there indefinitely, did I?"

"I can't remember; but I was certainly under the impression that you were staying for a few days, and you gave not the slightest hint that you intended to leave. I think you must enjoy behaving mysteriously."

"I'm simply a bad sleeper and an early riser. I can't bear lying in bed awake, my mind racing. . . ."

"But it shouldn't race. That's the trouble with you. You should just lie there peacefully, thinking great thoughts."

"You are very jocular today. Are you planning some mischief?"

"If I were, you are the last person I'd ever confide it in."

"Cyril Forbes is the man in your confidence. I know that. You must forgive me, Miss Kelly, if I became perhaps a little intense last night, but I had this overwhelming impression that you had betrayed my confidence. That's all."

"Don't, please, rake that up again. You were quite violent last night. You frightened me. Did you know that?"

"No. I'm sorry if I did. I was annoyed with you, I suppose. With me, anger is never long-lived. I can only remain in a dangerous mood for so long as it takes to swat a fly."

"All I can say is: I'm glad I'm not a fly."

Miss Kelly's spirits had soared with these exchanges. Mr Robinson could never be frivolous, would never be fun. She provided the light touch—she felt witty at the moment and flirtatious, and she didn't mind Mr Robinson being grave (and sometimes grim). It was not at odds with her ideal of a man and her first impressions of the sex.

He was looking at her now attentively and on the point of saying something, but she couldn't wait for it; her relief had gone to her tongue. She couldn't restrain it.

"Have you time to come up to the house for tea, Mr Robinson?"

"Thank you very much."

"Ten minutes' walk."

"You are forgetting; I have a car back there."

"All the better. We shall drive and save seven minutes."

When they arrived at the lane she felt embarrassed again. In spite of his denial and her bad sight, she was not convinced that Mr Robinson had been telling her the truth. She had become very familiar with his outline in the landscape, and even at a distance, no local man or itinerant would have brought his tall, trim figure to mind. Silence fell on them, and when they reached the road, Mr Robinson hailed the vision of his car, parked on the side, with an enthusiasm unusual for him.

Miss Kelly's first remark when they were seated and bound for home, a few hundred yards distant, revealed—although she was unaware of it—the course of her thoughts: "You know this part of Dublin, then. That's unusual; I always think of ourselves and the few houses on this side of the estuary as cut off from the world. It isn't the road to anywhere after the turn to Donabate. You must have known some of my neighbours?"

"In the days when I rode a motorcycle I used to explore the coast. I was very much on my own in those days—I've been always very much alone."

"I think it is very attractive here, but there's nowhere to go even to picnic. Were you interested in fishing?"

"A little. I've always been attracted by the sea. If I could have written, I'd have written about the sea. What wonderful stories the sea could tell; it must know so many secrets."

"You are a romantic after all. One would never have guessed it. We all are, I suppose, deep down. My brother, who was the most commonsense person you could imagine, got awfully excited whenever he saw a train. He had a passion for trains."

Outside the house, they sat for a moment to admire the view.

"It has been quite marvellous these last few days. You should have seen the estuary last night, when the sun was going down. Perhaps you'll have time, before you go. You haven't to rush away, I hope. Aggie won't be back until seven, or later. She always gives herself twice too much to do. Her family play upon her good nature. She won't listen to me. I tell her that what people set the highest price on is scarcity value. If they find you are available whenever required they take you for granted and only notice you when you fail to answer the bell."

"You are quite a philosopher, Miss Kelly."

"I have never met anyone who was in less need of that lesson, Mr Robinson. You are the most elusive man I have ever met."

Later, Miss Kelly heated the kettle while Mr Robinson sat in the drawing-room. She was a girl again as she laid the silver tray with the Crown Derby china, digestive biscuits, and the remains of one of Mrs Ridley's special fruit cakes. She carried in the tray.

"If I'd known you were coming, I'd have made you scones. Would you like bread and butter? And honey? Cyril gave . . ."

Mr Robinson must have seen her biting her lips.

"This is more than enough. That fruit cake looks very good. Do I hear the telephone?"

He did. It was Aggie to say that she was with her sister and had been called upon to baby-sit. She would not be back for dinner. Profuse in apologies, Miss Kelly cut them short. Would Aggie prefer to stay in Dublin for the night? "I shall be perfectly all right, my dear. I don't like the thought of you having to drive out here at all hours." Not later than ten o'clock she would be there, Aggie assured her. She did not say what both of them knew: she had no choice; her diabetic pills were at Miss Kelly's house.

"That was Aggie; she's been held up as usual by her remorseless family. I was going to make an omelette, I couldn't tempt you to take a share, I suppose? Then you could see the sun set."

"I would like to take you out somewhere for dinner."

"We would be much better off here. I shan't have to dress up. But you may have a very meagre meal. I can give you a decent bottle of wine, though. Here's the cellar key; you select a bottle for us. Michael invested in wine, poor man, the very year he died. I've been enjoying it ever since; but it's coming to an end."

Mr Robinson acquiesced in all her arrangements, and she, with a merry heart, set about preparing a meal. There was soup that needed only to be heated up, and which she liberally dosed with sherry. Omelettes, she prided herself on making. She had fruit and cream, good cheese and proper coffee.

The dining-room looked so cold and formal, she decided to

lay a small table in the library. She often used it when there was only a casual visitor or when she was alone. Mr Robinson was taking his time. He only appeared with a bottle of claret in his hand when his hostess was well forward with her preparations. She left him to uncork the wine before the library fire. She was singing to herself a tune of very long ago, "Tiptoe through the Tulips"; but she recollected herself in time when the soup boiled over.

Her manner was bright and attentive. She excelled herself in thoughtfulness, running back to the kitchen for chutney—home-made—one minute, and for celery the next. He begged her to forget about him and enjoy the meal.

"What makes you so restless this evening?"

She didn't know she was. It was her inadequacy as a cook. She kept the conversation going. After that early near-catastrophe she chose topics well removed from her recent life, but even so there were pitfalls in every path. The merits and demerits of television, for instance, led to references to plays on television, and plays were a mine-field she knew. As she pulled back from that one, her eyes turned involuntarily to the place on the shelves where she had replaced that fatal novel. Did Mr Robinson follow her glance? She thought so. But if he did, he was not bringing up the subject. There was in his manner what she could only interpret as a fixed resolve not to be led back into dangerous topics. They had eaten unfashionably early; when they rose from the table it was still daylight outside; but the sun was sinking, and through the bay window, facing west, the estuary was a sheet of flame.

It was Mr Robinson who suggested they should go out and enjoy the scene. Miss Kelly asked him, prickling at her daring, whether the evening reminded him of the last time he had visited this part of the country.

"It was in winter," Mr Robinson said, "and long after the sun had gone down."

She thought they would stroll in the grounds. There was a splendid view from the tennis lawn and rose garden; but Mr Robinson seemed to take for granted that they were going out in his car; she got in, just as she was.

94

"I've always done the driving," she thought to herself. She was in his hands now. She nestled comfortably in the imitation leather. Only eight o'clock.

Two hours at least before Aggie came back. Where would they go? She didn't enquire. She left everything to him. He drove very slowly as if looking for some landmark on the road-side; when they reached the lane she thought she had seen him measuring he halted, seemed to be considering, then drove down it and, half-way, drew in to the side and turned off the engine.

"You get a rotten view from here," she said.

"I want us to sit here, only for a few minutes, Miss Kelly. Do you mind?"

"Not at all. It just seems a pity to be missing—"

"I would rather look at you. There. Forgive me. It's uncanny."

"What is?"

"You. There. Beside me. I can't describe what I feel. It's as if I was being allowed to live again some enormously important moment in the past. You know how sometimes you get a sensation that it has all happened before. It has no other significance. It is only a trick of the brain, I believe, like the double exposure of a snapshot on a negative. In my case, it isn't a trick or an illusion. It was like this before; in another car certainly, and I was a youth, but you are the same. You haven't changed. Don't move, stay exactly as you are. Let me look at you. We sat like this. My arm was round you. May I? Your head fell over on my shoulder. That's right. We sat here together for three hours. It was longer than all the rest of my life that waiting time. Your face, your face felt so—"

"Mr Robinson, I don't understand a word you are saying. I'm not going to stay here any longer. I don't know who might go past at this hour of day. Please let me go."

And when he seemed oblivious to what she was saying, she struggled to free herself.

"Mr Robinson, please, my workman lives in the next cottage. You are hurting me. Let go. I shall get angry . . . Mr Robinson!"

She had seen in the driving mirror Tod and Mrs Donnelly.

They were walking slowly, in close conversation. Her shout aroused Mr Robinson. He seized the wheel as if suddenly alerted to danger. Miss Kelly opened the car door and stepped out almost on top of the Donnellys, who would have passed without seeing her if she had stayed where she was.

Miss Kelly apologised. Mrs Donnelly apologised. Tod Donnelly asked if there was anything wrong. Could he help? Miss Kelly said she was looking for money she had dropped out of her bag. The Donnellys offered to help to look for it. She had to persuade them to go on; she had abandoned the search. With instinctive tact the couple kept their eyes off Mr Robinson. He sat at the wheel, staring through the windscreen. When the Donnellys were out of sight, Miss Kelly returned to the car, but she did not get in.

"Goodbye to you," she said.

"Let me drive you home." His voice was gentle.

"Certainly not."

"You are doing me an injustice, Miss Kelly. I'd like to explain."

"I don't think any explanation is required. You saw what happened just now. It is all very well for you. I have to live here, Mr Robinson. I can't behave like a woman off the streets. I shall walk home."

He said nothing; but he certainly looked sad and crestfallen. He had held her very close, but he hadn't tried to kiss her and yet his grip was quite frantic; her ribs were sore. And he could hardly have intended to . . . Alone, in the house, if he had intentions of that sort . . . And what had he meant when he talked about this having happened before? Had he been in that lane with some girl in the past? He as much as said so. He had to wait for three hours with whoever it was beside him. "Your face," he said. "Your face felt so . . ." What did he mean! When he met her he told her she resembled his mother. In the car she was the girl he had been here with before. He was touched in the head. That was the only explanation, and she must not see him again or allow him to be alone with her.

The telephone was ringing when she opened her door, but it cut off before she was able to get to it. She threw herself into the chair beside the telephone; she was shivering, frightened. She reasoned with herself; the call was something unimportant, quite probably a wrong number; it could have had no significance, and yet missing it felt like losing an offer of help. But she was not in need of help. Aggie would be arriving quite soon. God bless her. What a comfort she was. So utterly unselfish always. The car episode had alarmed Miss Kelly much more than she realised at the time. In Donegal she had been prepared for Mr Robinson's advances; she had, she realised in retrospect, been even prepared *for the worst*, and when it didn't happen she had experienced, mixed with relief, a sense of deprivation, as on the occasion when Michael took her out of the theatre, he marching ahead, she glancing back at the scene on the stage. *The worst* seemed as if it was going to happen there then; but it couldn't have, not in 1949.

Today it had been different, eerie—she couldn't have explained—but she would not go through that again. She decided to give herself a little brandy; it would steady her up. She crossed the hall to the dining-room. She had left the front door open in her hurry, and when she was closing it, to make sure . . . she even put on the chain. A symbolic act. She was locking Mr Robinson out for ever. In the dining-room, she mixed herself quite a stiff brandy and soda. She would drink it quietly by the library fire, waiting for Aggie who, now the door was chained, did not seem so indispensable. The shivering fit had subsided.

In the library, Miss Kelly found Mr Robinson standing in front of the fire. She screamed, but no sound came.

"Look out," he said. The contents of the tumbler were spilling over the Chinese carpet, and Miss Kelly's hand was full of blood and broken glass. Mr Robinson took out a large white handkerchief, and when she had thrown the broken tumbler into the fire, he wrapped the bleeding hand in the clean linen.

"You had better wash that hand out carefully and put on some plaster," he said. "I'm sorry if I frightened you."

His ministering manner had cancelled out her shock at the apparition. He did sound kind and concerned. What a fright he had given her! Actually to break a tumbler!

97

"The door was open so I took the liberty of coming in. I am going away, and I couldn't go leaving you, of all people, under a false impression. I was afraid if I rang you might have refused to let me in."

"I'll see to my hand and then you may tell me whatever it is you want to say; but I'm expecting Mrs Fitzsimons at any moment."

"You are a fool," she told herself as she examined the scars on her palm. None was deep. She bandaged her hand quickly and came down with a sense of theatre. This then was Mr Robinson's farewell. She would be mad with herself after he had gone if she hadn't discovered his secret. There had been some woman in his life.

"Mrs Fitzsimons will be here at ten o'clock," she said, sitting down on the sofa. Mr Robinson, she directed to an armchair.

"How is your hand?"

"All right. I must have squeezed very hard. That never happened to me before."

"I've done it. I've crushed many a glass. But, then, you have soft hands. Mine . . ." He stretched them out. They were square, strong hands. He looked proud of them.

"They've done a lot of work," he explained.

"They nearly broke my ribs this afternoon. I am still waiting to hear what you thought you were doing."

"I think it was rather obvious."

"You were *not* making love to me, Mr Robinson."

"Yes and no. I was living through another experience. Only the light. That was different. When we were here before, it was dark, and pouring rain. It drummed on the roof of the car. I can hear it still, that and the watch ticking. It was against my ear."

Miss Kelly glanced at the clock. It was after nine. She had an hour. She must humour him. He was quite, quite mad. She knew that now. She had never been alone with a mad person before. Should she make some excuse and telephone to someone to come. Dr Groves or Father Barry. She had only to say it was very urgent. Either would come at once—to her. But he might suspect. He was keenly suspicious and watchful.

98

She had learned that already. Her best policy was to humour him.

"If you took my advice, you wouldn't think so much about the past. You seem to have been most unfortunate; but you are still a most attractive man. You will have no trouble in making new friends once you settle somewhere."

"But you don't understand. You see, I never really knew what happened that night, what was fact, what was dream. For days I had been mesmerised. I couldn't distinguish between my actions and the actions in the play, and I had no friend. There was no Sonia in my life. And I was under the influence of that evil man—I'll tell you his name. It doesn't matter now. Not after tonight, it won't—Max Morrison. Have you ever heard of him?"

"Yes I have; but I couldn't tell you anything about him."

"I'm sure your friend Cyril has mentioned his name."

"Most likely."

"Ever since the time my mother caught us in her bedroom, he wouldn't let me be; he kept on about her, what a nagging, stingy bitch she was, no use to anyone; he made me go back and demand money. 'If she doesn't give it, threaten her, frighten her out of her life. She'll pay you to keep out of her way. Tell her you'll put her to shame. Make an exhibition of yourself outside her house. Say you'll take her life.' That was how he used to talk to me after that awful day. I can still hear her wailing downstairs. I thought she had gone mad. And I see Max, on the bed, taking enormous pleasure in it—— Yes, indeed—and laughing in that wicked way he had. A cruel laugh, Miss Kelly."

"Mr Robinson, you are upsetting yourself. I beg you, for your own sake, try and forget that horrible time. It isn't good for you. Please believe me."

Mr Robinson got up at this and came and sat beside Miss Kelly on the sofa. He took one of her hands in his, but very gently, and his eyes had lost their manic expression. He looked suddenly very weary, and incurably sad.

"Help me. Only you can help me. I'll be as quick as I can if you'll hear me out. My mother was crying downstairs as if she was being beaten up. It was terrible to hear. I dressed as fast as I could. Max didn't move from the bed. 'Go down and tell that old

99

bag that she will bring in the Guards if she doesn't hold her noise,' he said.

"I did what I was told. I had no will to resist him in any event, but I was afraid my mother would alarm the neighbours. She was in the kitchen, and when she saw me, she shouted obscenities, every dirty name in the book. At the top of her voice. I begged her to stop. I said it had all been a lark. She was calling me such names, and the neighbours must have heard. I told her we were leaving. I wouldn't come back until she sent for me. I pleaded with her. But she kept it up, sometimes sobbing, sometimes using those filthy words. I never heard worse.

"Suddenly she stopped, only for a moment; Max stood in the door. Then she started off again; you can imagine what she said with both of us before her. Max walked up to her and said: 'Shut up, shut up, you old bitch.'

"She fairly let fly at that, and then he slapped her on the face, on each cheek, hard. She rocked. I ran forward and took his arm, but he had done the trick. She looked really frightened. I tried to say something to her, to dissociate myself from his brutality—although he did the only thing that would have stopped her. She had met her match. But I felt pretty bad as I followed him out. She was my mother, and I didn't like to think of her telling my father what she had seen. I knew she would. It would give her a perverse pleasure to tell him I was one of the things she said. And I still wanted my father to like me. He would never after this. I couldn't tell Max about my feelings. He despised all conventional sentiment. He hated families. He told me he could never resist an opportunity to break one up; he called them unnatural combinations, conspiracies. He said the only things that made him go to bed with women were money and the opportunity to break up a working marriage.

"You can see he would only have sneered at me for trying to defend my mother. 'I'd make short of her if she were my mother,' he said. When I was at rehearsals, I heard what Max was saying to me at home being repeated on the stage. In the play he acted the examining magistrate who knows Raskolnikov committed the crime and keeps playing cat and mouse with him until he confesses. You cannot conceive how extraordinary it was for me to listen to myself (as the student on the stage I mean) being cross-questioned by Max. If I had committed the crime it would have been because Max had persuaded me into doing it; and here he was on the stage acting for the police, trying to trick the truth out of me. And it was sinister, because I knew that if I did what he told me to do I could never rely on him for support. He had impressed me with his belief that we are all ruthless egoists under a thin protective coating, the result of centuries of organised hypocrisy. Morals had been invented to enable our exploiters to rule us. Great men insist on obedience to laws they don't observe themselves. Any fashionable Jesuit will assure his patron that there is one law in Heaven for the rich (if they are cultivated and hospitable) and another for the poor (upon whom subtleties are wasted). When is a crime not a crime? he used to say. Answer: When it has Government sanction. When is killing no murder? When it has Government sanction. That is how the world is run. It's up to each of us to decide whether it suits him to accept the convention or whether he has the guts to make laws for himself as great men always have. That is the crux of Raskolnikov's argument. Max as examining magistrate meets the case; but in private, with me, he was on Raskolnikov's side, and I used to say how can anyone himself determine whether he is one of the great ones entitled to make his own laws? If committing a crime was the test, then it would be a simple matter to empty the jails and put the convicts into Parliament. They, on that premise, are our rulers by natural right. He knocked down that argument. 'No one else can decide for you; you must have faith in yourself. Anyone in prison by definition is a failure; he hasn't been able to survive in a competitive environment. What is called a crime is a crime only if it serves no purpose. Only small criminals are sent to prison: look at Stalin. How glad any respectable Government would be to do business with him. Look at the way they panted to do business with Hitler, even after they knew about the night of the long knives and his Jewish persecutions. Believe me, all you need is courage, and you must make a start. That mother of yours has a house and a small stack of money, both of which you could use, and yet you can stand and let her call you to your face the most shocking

101

names. Really! I'm fairly seasoned, but your mother made me blush, dear. She is not—I repeat, not—a nice woman. I can't see any justification for her existence, and you are quite charming.'

"That is how he would talk when we were alone.

"The actress who was playing Sonia, the prostitute, objected because I was too intense at rehearsals. She said I put her off, staring at her. It wasn't because I lusted after her, not in the least. It was because I had never been loved, and I saw this girl, this beautiful character, who became a prostitute out of charity, was prepared to love the student after he had committed two murders. This novel, which should never have been published, taught that. *Crime and Punishment*: what a misleading title! You see Raskolnikov, poor, alone, starving, writing articles about crime; and then you see him after he has committed two murders and confesses; he is sent to Siberia, certainly, but Sonia goes with him. She will live with him in exile. He has work to do and food to eat. He has found love; he believes in God and the future. Is that punishment? I would not kill my mother or anyone for money; but if someone would admire me and love me for it, then there, certainly, was temptation. Max was urging me on, but would he admire me and love me if I did what he told me to? I didn't think so. He was only concerned to experiment with his power over people, to see how far he could push them. He began with me when he persuaded me to put on my mother's clothes. That was one step. He would have enjoyed hearing me abuse her; but I couldn't do that, any more than I could have struck her, whatever the provocation.

"And I knew Max would switch rôles. As soon as I became the criminal, I would meet him as the examining magistrate. He would enjoy playing with me. He would not be involved. I said to him:'Why don't *you* kill my mother and become Napoleon or Mussolini?' 'She is not in my way, my dear,' was his reply. His own parents lived in the country and he used occasionally to go down to see them. They sent him presents of chickens and vegetables. I never heard him plan to kill *them*. The only crimes he committed were petty thefts. There was a scene in the theatre when one of the staff lost a five pound note and swore it was in her bag when she put it down. Everyone suspected Max. But he didn't seem aware. I knew it was he because the landlord had become unpleasant about the rent one day, and Max paid him the next, and there was nowhere else he could have found the money in the interim.

"Why did I stay with him? I had nowhere else. He professed to like me. I had no will. And I was hypnotised by this madman, Dostoevsky. I would burn that book, Miss Kelly, if I were you.

"I'll get it now. Let us do this together."

Not waiting for her assent, he jumped to his feet and went straight to the place on the shelf where the offending novel, pushed quickly into place, stuck out a little.

"Don't burn my book, Mr Robinson. There is no sense at all in what you are doing."

And as he poked at the fire, she snatched at the novel, but he held it out of her reach.

"There," he said, when a flame spurted up and he put the book firmly in, at the risk of burning his hand.

Miss Kelly seized the tongs and pulled the book out. Fear had vanished when she had to protect her property.

"You shouldn't have done that," Mr Robinson said, shaking his head sadly. "When I think of the misery that book has caused."

"Not to sensible people. The cover of the book is ruined. Oh, dear! Mr Robinson! Have you taken leave of your senses?"

Miss Kelly nursed the injured book; fear had been displaced for the moment by a sense of outrage. And Mr Robinson rebuked, looked abashed and no longer sinister.

"You must forgive me; that wicked book ruined my life once and when I saw it being used against me now—"

"I don't know what you mean," Miss Kelly interrupted, "and in any event, it couldn't justify your throwing any book of mine into the fire. I've put up with a good deal, but if you think that entitles you to destroy my property, I would like to tell you that I can't see any difference between what you have just done and trying to steal it. Frankly, I don't."

"You would never have taken down that book if Cyril Forbes hadn't mentioned it. He has only Max's account of what happened; and Max was only concerned to keep himself right

103

with people like the Forbeses who were rich and entertained him."

"Cyril didn't mention the book; he gave me its name when I told him the plot. That's all. He didn't mention you or Max whatever-his-name-is. I can't remember his ever talking about either of you, and I don't see why he should begin now."

Mr Robinson made no reply to this; he was staring very hard at Miss Kelly, and she knew from the expression in his eyes that his mind was no longer on the book. He was back at the beginning.

"Cyril Forbes knew my mother, or, rather, his parents did; has he never remarked on the resemblance?"

"Mine to her, you mean? Never."

"That is extraordinary."

"You are forgetting that he has known me always and when he saw your mother, she was a different generation. I was in my teens."

"Still."

"I think you are rather obsessed with this alleged resemblance. If I were to ask Cyril what your mother looked like, he would only have a vague impression. It's how long ago?"

"Nearly forty years. You were a child. Were you in a convent at the time? Abroad somewhere?"

"When? What *are* you talking about?"

"When my mother died."

"I don't know when your mother died. I don't know anything about you, Mr Robinson, except what you've told me. All I know is that I thought we were going to be friends, and you've behaved in the most extraordinary manner. I'd rather say no more about it. Mrs Fitzsimons will be back at any moment, and if you don't mind, I'd prefer it if she didn't find you here."

"I'm going away tomorrow."

"Then you ought to have a good night's sleep beforehand."

"You are being unkind. I am a very unhappy man. You can help me. You are the only person who can."

"How? If it's a question of . . ." Miss Kelly coloured. She could only think of money, and that, certainly, was not what was worrying Mr Robinson. He did not notice her embarrassment.

"I had given up all hope of ever discovering the truth. I came back to Ireland on the merest impulse; and then without any previous plan, by the merest chance, I go to that guest house, and almost on my arrival, I see you. If I could believe in Providence, I'd say it sent me there, because I knew when I saw you that I had been the victim—I can't say of a conspiracy; Max didn't conspire against me—but of a vast hallucination. There was no one to help me. My father didn't understand; he did what he could at the time. I do believe that. Afterwards he went away. I started letters to him, hundreds, but never finished them. Then I heard he was dead; his lawyers wrote to me in Australia. He left whatever he had in trust for me. After I die, it goes to the Dublin Zoo. Nice touch, that! He only knew half the story, and he didn't believe it—I know—although he supported me. Before I could convince him, I had to convince myself, Miss Kelly. That damned book had hypnotised me. I couldn't believe my own truth. Without the play, the book wouldn't have done it; I could not have identified myself completely with a character in fiction; but when I saw him on the stage, when he was palpable—that was when I was taken over. I stood watching *myself*, night after night. My father came to see me. My mother told him about finding us in her bedroom. I knew she would. She probably told him about the ten pound note as well. He called on me at Max's place—"

Miss Kelly suddenly stood up.

"Mr Robinson, I'm very sorry, but I really must ask you to go now. And I do think it's for the best. You are upsetting yourself to no purpose. When you go away, you must forget about all this. I am very sorry that I should have been the cause of your distress."

"On the contrary. I believe that you have saved my reason. You've no idea what it is like to live for nearly forty years in a past that is mostly a dream. If I believed in God, I'd say He sent you to help me sort it out. Why should I be a victim of my dreams?"

"I can't change your dreams, Mr Robinson."

"You will if you listen. Give me half an hour."

"My friend—"

"I have my car outside. You could leave a note for her."

"It's far too late, and in any case . . ."

"I was carried away this afternoon. I didn't mean to touch you. I forgot who you were. I'm past the age when I make advances to young women in motor cars—for heaven's sake!"

"You nearly succeeded in making me look ridiculous. I'm not a young woman, Mr Robinson. I don't want to be made a laughing stock among my neighbours."

The telephone rang in another room. Miss Kelly pretended not to hear.

"You completely misunderstood me. Did I hear the telephone?"

Miss Kelly would have said "No", but he continued to listen.

"Will you excuse me?"

Full of misgivings, she left the room. A boy's voice answered her.

"This is Frank. Aunt Aggie has had to go to hospital. It isn't serious, but the doctor says she must stay in for a couple of days. She asked me to ring up and explain. She will ring you up herself in the morning."

"Where is she? This is terrible. She seemed perfectly well today."

The youth assured her there was no cause for alarm. Slight palpitations. Nothing more.

"I'm terribly upset." Miss Kelly spoke with conviction. She was. She was sorry and terrified. Much more terrified than sorry. She did not have to tell Mr Robinson; but she would now insist that he left her at once. If only she could think up some convincing lie. She was never able to do that. Not even in an emergency. Not even in an emergency such as this. She came away from the telephone. Mr Robinson was standing at the open door.

"I came to say goodbye," he said.

Miss Kelly was unable to conceal her relief.

"I hope you will have a safe journey, and I'm sure that when you settle down in England, you'll be much happier. This country has changed out of all knowledge since you lived here."

"England, they tell me, even more so."

106

"I'm sure there are pleasant places still. Have you thought of East Anglia? Charming villages, and small houses, not too expensive. Keep well away from London."

Her talk was a conjuror's patter while she performed the trick of getting Mr Robinson off the premises. It ran out inevitably, and she was left impaled on his stare.

"Had you a hat?"

He never wore one, she knew, and she knew he knew she knew. It was the politest form in which she could ask him to get out, and she was baffled when he continued to stand there gazing at her.

"I couldn't help hearing you had bad news just now. I hope your friend hasn't been taken ill."

"She has been delayed. She is on her way. That was her nephew to reassure me. A very nice boy, going to be an accountant. Lots of brains. So hard to find jobs, though, they tell me."

"You sounded very much upset. I'm afraid I was the cause. I live so much inside myself, Miss Kelly, that I forget about the world sometimes. Since I've met you, I haven't felt alone. Believe me, you have done more for me in these last few days than any doctor who has ever tried to help me. I can never be grateful enough. If we never meet again, I'd like you to know that you have been my good angel."

He bowed and walked out as a king might to his execution. Miss Kelly stood without moving until the door shut behind him, until she heard the engine of a car and the scramble of loose gravel under the tyres as it drove away. Then she ran to the window of the dining-room and watched the lights creep down the drive until they were hidden by the trees.

Part 3

MISS KELLY HAD made no promise to Mr Robinson where Aggie was concerned; and on the morning following his departure, Mrs Fitzsimons, in the private patients' wing of St Vincent's Hospital, after a presentation of grapes (purple, 1 lb) and the current number of *Country Life*, and an enquiry as to the exact state of her health, was regaled with a very full account of the events of the previous day. Her attempts at diversion ("It reminds me exactly of what happened to a niece of mine at Parknasilla") were properly scouted; Miss Kelly was not to be stayed (there were times when she could have hit the patient) and when she had done, Aggie expressed the deepest contrition.

"I shall never forgive myself for letting you down. My *silly* old heart. That man Robinson is obviously off his head. I didn't know *what* you were going to tell me. To have been alone in the house with him, and knowing I wasn't coming and his listening to the telephone conversation. Oh, my dear! Do take some of the grapes. I can't possibly eat them all. The man my niece had the trouble with in Parknasilla wasn't mad; but one doesn't like a girl to be subjected to that sort of experience. It might easily—"

"I hope you didn't read more into that than I told you, Aggie," Miss Kelly interrupted briskly. "What was disconcerting was his manner, the tone of voice, and his talking to me as if I were somebody else. He didn't *do* anything to me, you understand."

"Of course not, dear. But you couldn't tell what a man like that *might* do. One simply can't afford to take risks nowadays. That's what I said to Peggy when she came back from Parknasilla—"

Miss Kelly looked at her watch.

"I shall be late for lunch if I don't get moving," she said. It had been on the tip of her tongue to invite her friend for the weekend, but she wouldn't now. She would try to persuade Cyril to come. The subject of Mr Robinson could be brought up indirectly. She wouldn't tell anything, but she would listen. She was entitled, after all she had been through, at least to that.

His abruptness and sudden departures had been her chief cause of complaint against him; but nothing became him like his final exit. Having worked her up to a state of terror by his theatrical behaviour, the relief of his going—his timing and the handsomeness of his curtain line—left her more fascinated by him than ever. In her account of those happenings on the last day to Aggie she had given the story a colouring as might the sub-editor of a newspaper to whom it has been handed by a cub reporter.

Mr Robinson's behaviour in the motor car, as if he was with another person, was unlike anything in Miss Kelly's experience, and she had no point of reference. When she was describing it to Aggie, she edited it very slightly because she had interpreted it as a fit of uncontrollable passion aroused by the memory of some former occasion when Mr Robinson's desires had proved too strong in a similar situation. She reminded him of his mother, he had said that often enough, but in the car—and he had had the nerve to suggest a second jaunt late at night!—he had behaved like a lover. She had read somewhere that men often marry women who remind them of their mothers. Possibly that explained his conduct. She belonged to the type that fatally attracted Mr Robinson, and being so very like his mother, she attracted him that much more strongly than the others. There had been some woman once who had gone to his head in the same way. What had happened to her? Mr Robinson seldom spoke about women; he gave an impression of rugged celibacy. Endlessly playing chess or looking up timetables when he wasn't herding sheep, Mr Robinson's years in Australia conjured up a picture of a latter-day Desert Father. Once before, perhaps, he had seen a girl who reminded him vividly of his mother. If he behaved towards her as he had behaved when he called on Miss Kelly, it was not to be wondered at if she discouraged his suit.

Instead of congratulating herself on a lucky escape from a lunatic, Miss Kelly found herself the victim of retrospective jealousy. Who was this other girl? How far had *she* gone with Mr Robinson? Had there been one incident in a car when Mr

112

Robinson forgot himself and then made his excuse that the lady had reminded him of his mother, or had this been one scene among many? Miss Kelly blamed herself for the way she had handled her admirer. When she had spoken up—after he threw the book in the fire—Mr Robinson had come to heel. (She liked that expression, there was something dog-like about Mr Robinson. He had the noble appearance of a hound, and his eyes had the faraway look a gun-dog's has, and he sometimes showed his teeth, dog-fashion.) He was certainly odd; this business about his mother had affected him very much, and the behaviour of his friend—but she did not want to think about that—all these experiences of his youth had scarred him. He had seen her as the woman who could mend his life by taking the place his mother had failed him in, and if she had agreed with Aggie that she had had a lucky escape, she could not get Mr Robinson out of her mind. She thought of nothing else.

Aggie did her own editing of her friend's story: she was concerned, because she saw the episode as an example of menopausal delusion. While at times she had deplored the Kelly arrogance—it had deprived her friend of the best part of woman's experience—she would have expected it to keep her out of scrapes of this sort. The story had, to her ears, something sordid and unhealthy about it. And what alarmed her was a conviction that Miss Kelly, so far from learning from the experience, had only been excited by it, and was keener than ever on this strange person.

"I'd try to get *that* gentleman out of my mind, if I were you," Aggie had advised.

"Oh, he isn't on my mind, I assure you. I hope I never go through a day like yesterday again as long as I live. I had to tell someone. And you must promise never to repeat to a soul what I've told you. You have seen the way a story gets distorted when it's passed around."

"You know me, dear. I'm like cement where secrets are concerned. You couldn't dig them out of me."

They had parted in perfect amity, Aggie all concern; her friend heroic, begging her to obey her doctor's whims; her health was what mattered most.

113

A letter at home announced the return of the Ridleys on Thursday. It was full of respect and affection and mis-spelling, the sort of letter Miss Kelly liked, and a miracle in these rough times.

The way was clear. Cyril said he would enjoy a weekend. His back was better.

"I want to be kept up to date with your love-life," he said.

"You haven't improved," Miss Kelly answered archly.

"It's too late," he replied.

This and the promised return of the reliable Ridleys was enormously comforting. The world was on its feet again. Even so, Miss Kelly found her mind returning to Mr Robinson; she played back every scene and tried to interpret it, always with a sense of opportunity lost, of having been given a glimpse of a strange country, of dark forests and dangerous animals; it had exercised a fascination so powerful that she had been frightened by her own helplessness.

She was looking forward greatly to Cyril's visit; in the past she had often grumbled to herself at the complacency with which he expected her to drive nearly twenty miles to fetch him, when he had a car of his own and a driver; but today she started off soon after breakfast; she was wonderfully eager to see Cyril; he had assumed a new interest and importance. Was she bound by her promise? It was absurd if he could fill in the gaps to feel bound by what she had promised when she was too frightened to refuse. And yet she felt a curious loyalty to Mr Robinson; he had stirred something in her; he had given her what she had never known in all her life—a sense of mystery, of possibilities of strange excitements. It was an enormous relief that he had gone; but life without him looked empty and boring. If Cyril had suddenly become exciting, it was solely on Mr Robinson's account. She could think of nothing else.

"I wasn't expecting you so early," he said, with the very slightest suggestion of reproof; but he was dressed and shaven and the newspaper beside his chair had the appearance of having been thoroughly gone over. "Mrs Robinson will give us coffee. Sit down there quietly. I must make out a little list, and then I'll be ready to go."

Mrs Robinson, who had been hovering, sped to the kitchen.

She, too, had become possessed of a new importance—with that name! The most prosaic name possible, Miss Kelly would have said, in all the years that she had known Cyril's housekeeper. Not now.

"What did Mrs Robinson's husband do when he was alive?" she asked, never in twenty years having felt the least interest in anything about the decent woman.

"In the drapery trade. A widower. He left her a step-daughter of about her own age, a rather grim-visaged female with whom she spends Christmas. What makes you ask?"

"I was just wondering."

"Why *now*? You've known Mrs Robinson for twenty-two years. Are you making your will? If so, I shall take it in bad part if I'm cut out for Mrs Robinson."

Mrs Robinson brought in coffee; then Cyril insisted on showing Miss Kelly around the garden. He was rather proud of it, and this was a ritual. But today she had more exciting thoughts in her mind, and she wasn't able to conceal them. She enthused too much. He knew her. He wondered. Visits to Miss Kelly differed only in minute detail; sometimes there were guests to lunch or dinner, or Cyril was included in a neighbour's invitation. His coming, indeed, was often a signal for local entertainment; a single man with sociable habits being something of a rarity in those parts.

"The Cobleys are expecting us to lunch tomorrow," Miss Kelly told him, "and we are going for drinks to the Brown-Thomas's this evening."

"We are living off the country, I see. Well, I'm all in favour of that."

"What has you in this cynical mood, Cyril?" she enquired when they were drinking their pre-lunch martinis. Cyril had insisted on fixing them, assuring her it was an art she had never acquired.

"What's the matter with *you*? That's what interests me. Are you keeping something back? Has Mr Robinson turned up again? I'd love to know his Christian name? Or has he not got one? My Mrs Robinson is called Bridget Christina. I'd have never known that if I hadn't to buy stamps for her social insurance."

"Oh, Mr *Robinson*. For a moment I didn't know who you were talking about. He did as a matter of fact. A very strange creature. I'm not sorry he has gone."

"He sounded very nutty to me; did you find out anything more about him?"

"Not really. He has been in Australia for years. His father was a solicitor in Dublin. He was connected with the Phoenix Theatre. But I gather he didn't get very far. He got on very badly with his mother; and she died. I think he has never recovered from a sense of guilt, but from what he told me, she was not a kind mother."

"And he has gone away?"

"I thought I should never get him to go, to be strictly truthful; but he said such nice things when he was leaving, I felt I had misjudged him."

"I think you are well rid of him. I must tell Mrs Ridley to keep a close watch on you in case he comes back again. I don't trust you with Mr Robinson, my dear."

Miss Kelly blushed. It did not become her as it started in her chest. Cyril was having trouble with a ribbon of green lettuce in his prawn cocktail and did not observe the effect of his teasing.

When the conversation had drifted what Miss Kelly considered a safe distance, she asked Cyril if he remembered someone who acted in the Phoenix Theatre called Max Morrison. He paused, fork in mid-air, and then said, "He acted a bit; he did a bit of everything; what made you think of him?"

"Nothing. I was trying to remember the names of the people who acted in those days."

"This is Mr Robinson's influence. I certainly don't remember *him*."

Miss Kelly was about to say that Mr Robinson remembered Cyril, but hesitated because that might be a betrayal of her promise: what exactly *had* she promised? Inconveniently, Cyril knew about him, and it was impossible to avoid the subject; neither did she want to. In fact she wanted Cyril to talk about nothing else.

"Did Max have a part in *Crime and Punishment*, can you remember?"

116

"I don't know. I didn't see it. How could I possibly remember? Why are you so interested in Max Morrison all of a sudden?"

"I was wondering what happened to him. I believe he married someone and lives in England. If he is still alive."

"You've answered your own question."

"I meant: he doesn't act now. I never hear his name."

"He wasn't an actor; he could do a little of anything. He was arty and acquisitive, posing as a nineties figure, a left-over from the *Yellow Book*, actually a crook and a sinister one."

"Did he live with anyone?"

"My dear, what has got into you? Max was by no means a nice person, as I've tried discreetly to hint. When he left the country, there were cheques bouncing off the walls of every bank in Dublin."

"I hope he hadn't given you one of them. I never met him, did I?"

"How can I answer that question? But I'd say he had cleared out before you began to go to parties."

"I might have met him at your house."

"Who told you he ever came to my house?"

"I only assumed . . ."

"Don't assume anything of the kind. I'd forgotten this person's existence; he was a thief, with a very unsavoury reputation. I don't know why you insist on spoiling a perfectly good lunch by going on about him so."

"I didn't mean to upset you."

"You haven't upset me in the least."

But she had; he sulked all afternoon, gave her short answers; and she was relieved when the time came for the cheerful Brown-Thomas's to take him over, feed him well, and gradually win him back to his giggling, naughty self.

She had learned her lesson, and although she was determined to find out as much as she could about Max Morrison as well as Mr Robinson—nothing else in the world interested her at the moment—she had already learned that Mr Robinson's picture of Max was not exaggerated. He was a bad person, and Cyril was obviously and naturally annoyed at her extreme lack of tact. She had always had a single-track mind; when she was involved in anything, she refused to think or talk about anything else. She would have to put a brake on her tongue until she had returned Cyril to Killiney, then she would begin her investigations. She understood Cyril's reaction, but she was surprised that he didn't remember Mr Robinson's living with Max. Surely that would have been known to all his acquaintances, and as Cyril was so teasing and curious about Mr Robinson, why had he not pricked up his ears when she mentioned him in connection with Max? Why hadn't he even said "There was some youth whose name may have been Robinson"? But he hadn't; he had very definitely given the impression he was hearing about Mr Robinson for the first time. In one way, that was comforting. Mr Robinson had represented himself as a victim; and it looked as if he had been; and Miss Kelly felt hugely relieved by this because, even though his mysteriousness had thrilled her, she wanted to know that underneath it, however eccentric, someone of whom she could approve lay hidden.

Wherever she found herself and whatever company she was in, Miss Kelly never lost an opportunity of enquiring about Max Morrison. Nobody knew who she was talking about, and even though she felt like Sherlock Holmes when she consulted back copies of newspapers in the public library, all she learned was that he gave an "entirely convincing" performance as the examining magistrate in *Crime and Punishment*. In other plays, he tended to be included among the recipients of the critic's consolation prizes at the end of his notice. Still, it was something to see in print the evidence of his existence. Miss Kelly saw no reference to any Robinson in the cast lists, but then he had been only one of the crowd. Her researches were not productive, but they gave her life a sense of purpose.

One afternoon, after a committee meeting, the ladies who were organising a sale for a worthy cause stayed on in the hotel for refreshment. Miss Kelly brought the subject of the Phoenix Theatre up by reminding one of her colleagues, who lived in Killiney, that it was a district in which Max Morrison, the actor, once boasted several friends. As always, she drew a blank; if she hadn't and found herself having to explain her interest she would have claimed a friend in common and hinted that he had suffered at Max's hands. This would be a certain way of extracting all the dirt available. That she was dredging for dirt was apparent even to herself. But if she discovered someone who knew Max she might then be able to lead the conversation on to Mr Robinson. Mr Robinson was never out of her thoughts for long; and he haunted her dreams. Usually he was looking at her reproachfully. Sometimes he was confused with the statesman he resembled, and then he was either addressing meetings or on television and she had always a humiliating part to play in these dreams. Sometimes Mr Robinson became frightening and threatened her. Once he made love to her. They were under Slieve League in the grassy hollow. She had her eyes shut; he was kissing her. She had no clothes on; but how they came off she was not told. He lay on top of her, crushing her into the ground. She woke up sweating, and put her hands under the pillow.

Nothing of this kind had ever happened to Miss Kelly in fifty-two years. As she was leaving the committee meeting, one of the members asked for a lift; it was raining and Miss Kelly's car was at the door. In the course of the conversation she said to Miss Kelly, "I heard you asking about Max Morrison. Is he still in the land of the living?"

Miss Kelly said she thought he was. Her new acquaintance, much older than herself, felt her way with finesse, and when she discovered that Miss Kelly wasn't a friend, described him as a blackguard who had married the daughter of a friend of hers, spent her money, and then deserted her. The girl had since died. Miss Kelly now had her opportunity, and said that he had treated a friend of hers very badly.

"A man or a woman?"

"Very much a man," Miss Kelly said.

"Max was a raging pansy when I knew him."

Miss Kelly sat in the car—she had gone out of her way to drop her passenger home—and listened to an account of Max's youth, which didn't interest her very much because she had thought for a moment she had met someone at last who knew Mr Robinson. But she wasn't going to go without making sure.

"Did you ever meet a friend of Max's called Robinson? He shared his flat for a time."

"That wouldn't recommend him. I don't remember the name. But, then, I didn't move in those circles. Max's family happened to come from my part of the country, and the girl he ruined was the daughter of a friend. Stage-struck, very silly and spoilt. I was sorry for her parents."

Miss Kelly declined an invitation that she was not meant to accept, and returned home in a perplexed state of mind. Max was real—in some ways too real—but Mr Robinson remained a mystery. It was almost as if he were a figment of her own imagination. And, as he said, he became confused between his own identity, the student in the play, and the figure in his dreams, so did Miss Kelly begin to wonder if she, too, might not be suffering from hallucinations. She continued to dream about Mr Robinson. So frequently that she became unable to distinguish between her waking and sleeping life. Night was so much more exciting than day. When a large envelope came to her, posted in London, addressed in a painful script, she knew at once this was from Mr Robinson, and she had to take thought to make quite sure that this was day and she was awake and this was an actual letter. She went into the library and took the telephone receiver off the hook before she settled down to read. Her hands were trembling and her eyes ran so fast over the opening lines she was obliged to go back to the beginning. There was no address and no date.

Dear Miss Kelly,

I should be obliged if you would undertake a commission for me. When I was in Ireland, I made several attempts to get in touch with a retired police detective, Dermot Lynch. He lives at a house called Seamount in Delgany, Co Wicklow. I believe that he wishes to avoid me or his family may have stood in my way. He has in his possession a file on a case in which I was concerned. It is, of course, the property of the State, but I am prepared to pay £2,000, I cannot afford more, if he will give me the file. I am only concerned that it will not be left to fall into irresponsible hands when Lynch is dead. He

120

won't let it out of his own while he is alive because he would be ordered to hand it back to the proper authorities. If he will not sell it to me I am quite satisfied to pay the same amount on the condition that he burns the file in the presence of yourself or myself. I have reason to believe that he is avoiding me, but he might be persuaded to take a more favourable view of the proposition if you were the intermediary.

I found him very sympathetic; at a time when he could have made my life intolerable, he showed himself humane. So much so that I thought of him as a friend. This led to my downfall, as he can explain; but he was doing only his duty and I can't hold it against him.

I have no permanent address, but I will call you on the telephone a fortnight from now and find out how you have fared. I made the mistake of writing to Lynch myself. If you take my advice you will call on him some afternoon; unless age has greatly changed him, he will be affable, and I have a hunch that you will succeed where I have failed.

I have found out where Max is living, by the way. His wife died long since, leaving him well-to-do. I shall call on him in due course; but before that I am determined to clear up the matter at the Irish end. And I know, Miss Kelly, that you will not refuse to help me.

"Henry Robinson" at the letter's end looked absurdly imper-sonal and somehow pathetic, as if, instead of a signature, he had made his mark. Miss Kelly read the letter over several times. Her satisfaction in getting it was only marginally diminished by Mr Robinson's failure to convey any interest in herself except insofar as she could assist him. But his reliance on her was flattering. In any event, she was determined to do what he wished and when he rang up be able to tell him the file was either in her possession or in Mr Lynch's fire—because her plan was to draw her own cheque and let Mr Robinson recoup her. Nor-mally reluctant to put her name to any cheque, Miss Kelly was in a fever to see it on this one. She plotted and planned and had no wish to consult anyone. Aggie, when they met, enquired if there was anything on her mind, so obvious was her

121

preoccupation; and when she asked if by any chance she had heard from Mr Robinson, Miss Kelly said she had, and looked more mysterious than ever.

She traced the retired detective in the telephone directory, and after lunching with Cyril, drove on to Delgany to spy out the land. Seamount was one of a row of new bungalows. Miss Kelly was reminded of the search for Mr Robinson's father's cottage in Donegal. How angry he had been when she had spoken to the woman in the shop; it deterred her now from making enquiries about her quarry. Who would she have to contend with? A wife? A devoted daughter? A dragon housekeeper? She would have liked to know. She saw a shop selling newspapers and light groceries, and went in. What was more natural than to say she was looking for his house?

There was a pleasant-looking elderly woman talking to the shopman. When she had finished, Miss Kelly asked him if he knew where a Mr Dermont Lynch lived. This was met with a laugh.

"Is it the Superintendent? Well you have come on the right day. This is Mrs Lynch." Miss Kelly found herself confronted by kind, shrewd eyes.

"Did you want to see my husband?" Mrs Lynch enquired.

All Miss Kelly, who looked so unexceptionable, had to say was, "If he is not too busy," and they would have walked back to the Lynchs' house without any embarrassment; but Miss Kelly had been over-impressed by Mr Robinson's account of his difficulties and could not believe that access would be so easy. She looked haughty while she searched her unhelpful wits for inspiration.

"I hadn't intended calling today," she said.

"He's up at the house now."

Miss Kelly felt she was being rushed; she wanted to think out her strategy; if she was at a loss at this stage, she wouldn't be able to open the subject when she met the former detective. But here was his wife, friendly and smiling; it was stupid not to take advantage of the accident. It never occurred to her that she was not an object of interest or that her appearance suggested that the greatest matter she could possibly be concerned with was the loss of her handbag.

Awkwardly, she accepted the offer, and on the short walk uttered the usual banalities about the weather and the way everywhere had changed so much one couldn't recognise once familiar places. When they arrived at the bungalow, Miss Kelly took note, unconscious of the condecension in her manner, of the neat lawn in front of the house, islanded with rose beds. Decent and tidy and unpretentious was her verdict on the small hall, and when Mrs Lynch opened an inner door, Miss Kelly took in at a glance the carpet of a shade and pattern that she associated only with shop windows, walls covered with family photographs, and in every corner of the room, a surprising number of books. She was always agreeably surprised to discover evidence of efforts at self-improvement.

"Daddy," said Mrs Lynch, "a lady wants to see you," and then, at the door, "I don't think I caught your name."

"Kelly."

"Mrs Kelly," added Mrs Lynch, leaving her face to face with an elderly man in an armchair.

"Excuse me, but I find it very hard to get up," he said. "Would you like to take that chair. This one has dog's hairs on it. And to what do I owe this pleasure, Mrs Kelly?"

"Miss Kelly."

"I beg your pardon. *Miss* Kelly."

His manners she approved, and he had a kindly humorous look, reminding her of the local doctor in her childhood. She felt suddenly at ease.

"I don't know where to begin," she whinnied.

"Anywhere you like," he said, looking paternal.

"I would like first to explain my own position. I don't know anything about the background of what I am going to mention or about the other persons concerned. I was on holiday, taking a rest cure really, recently, and I met a Mr Robinson. We became friends and he came to call on me at my house at Swords. He had been out of the country for nearly forty years, I gathered. I never got a full account of what happened but it was clear he had been in difficulties with the police.

"Only the other day I received a letter, which I have here, and you may read it. He says he has been trying to get in touch with

123

you without success. Perhaps you had better read it for yourself; and then you can tell me how you feel about his proposal.

"I want to help Mr Robinson. I'm convinced that his only chance of leading any sort of normal life is to lay this ghost that haunts him, the memory of injustice and disgrace. What makes my part difficult is that I have never been told, in so many words, what it is that is so much on Mr Robinson's mind. He says that you were the only person who treated him kindly when he was in trouble."

While Miss Kelly was talking, her listener looked interested and alert. When she had finished, he said, "I know very well what you are talking about; but where does the name *Robinson* come in?"

"You'll see it at the end of that letter to me. My friend's name is Robinson."

The former detective said nothing, but he took the letter and read it through.

"May I keep this?" he said when he had finished.

"My letter?"

"I'd like to add it to the file. Miss Kelly, will you take the advice of a much older man, who knows all about this matter and has been in it from the beginning, and have nothing more to do with Mr Robinson. He is not the sort of man I'd recommend to you as a friend, and I'd keep out of his business. I'm sure a lady in your position has her own social circle. I can promise you Mr Robinson will be no addition to it. Leave him to me, and if he rings up, say you called on me, and if he wants to write to me again, I'll answer his letter."

In surroundings such as this, Miss Kelly would always see herself dictating the tone of the discussion, and in an effort to gain control, she blurted out that she had her cheque book with her and would like to purchase the file for two thousand pounds. The ex-detective neither jumped at the offer nor showed any resentment, but asked why she would do anything so foolish.

"Mr Robinson is prepared to pay that much. You saw it in the letter. I am doing this because I am convinced it is the only step that will give him any peace of mind after forty years. In any event he is prepared to pay, and whatever you may think of him, I am convinced he has the money and can afford to give it back to me."

"But, my dear Miss Kelly, the file isn't my property. I can't sell it or destroy it. I happen to have it here, but back to the Department of Justice it must go, sooner or later, and in the light of our discussion, it strikes me that it can't go back too soon."

"I'm prepared to add a thousand to the sum."

"You are trying to bribe me."

"Certainly not. I can see your objection to having the file in circulation, but if it is destroyed, no one will ever be the wiser. Does anyone know you have it?"

"Nobody is interested. This has been a closed case for most of your lifetime."

"Very well, will you accept my offer?"

"No. And the fact that you can make it worries me."

"Please don't misunderstand me. I realise that these papers are interesting; and I don't see why you should give them up without recompense. If it is on the high side that is only because it matters so much to Mr Robinson. He is morbidly sensitive on the subject. I should be interested to see what the file shows about a man called Max Morrison. I got the impression from Mr Robinson that he was the cause of all his misfortunes, and he is still alive."

Mr Lynch, like so many men when Miss Kelly talked earnestly to them, seemed more interested in his own thoughts. He was obviously thinking hard. He held his chin, then looked away, then turned to her.

"You may read the file, Miss Kelly; but you will have to do that here. You can come whenever you please. If I'm not here, my wife will look after you. When you have read the file, you will be in a better position to assess the situation."

"You won't accept my offer?"

"Read the file, Miss Kelly."

"But you don't appreciate my position. I am not doing this out of vulgar curiosity. I'm here solely on Mr Robinson's account."

"That can't be true."

"I *beg* your pardon."

"I don't know anybody connected with the case of that name."

"You have his letter in front of you."

"I recognise the handwriting."

"Well, whose is it?"

"Nevil Norval's."

"And who, pray, is Nevil Norval?"

"His name is on the file that you have been trying to buy from me. And there is nobody called Robinson on the file."

"Didn't Mr Robinson try to get in touch with you very recently?"

"No, Miss Kelly. There was a Mr Norval looking for me; but I avoided meeting him. Don't let it distress you. I am glad you came to see me. I shouldn't be at home, if I were you, if Mr Robinson calls on you again."

Miss Kelly was surprised at her own coolness. She felt quite extraordinarily calm. She had heard that some people were like that when they heard the most appalling news, a death or all their money lost.

"I don't quite know *what* to say."

"You needn't say anything; but if you want to read the file, you may do so. It's a matter for yourself. But I think it is my duty to let you know in what sort of country you have been travelling recently. Your Mr Robinson was trying to see me, as you say, and to tell you the truth, Miss Kelly, I was very curious to see him again after so many years; but I was in the doctor's hands, and when I told him who the caller was, he forbade him the house. My ticker gives me trouble, and I was advised not to get excited. I've had enough for today, by the same token. What I would suggest, if you don't mind, is that you come back another day. I'll let you see the file, and I'd like to hear about Mr Robinson, if you don't mind telling me. I never expected him to appear again, and I'm interested, to say the least."

"I do hope I haven't tired you. I didn't mean to descend on you like this without notice. I just happened—"

"That's quite all right. You come back whatever day suits

126

you. I'm usually at home, but if you want to make sure I will be, I'll give you my telephone number."

"What a lot of books you have," Miss Kelly said on her way out, betraying surprise. Then she glanced about her to see if there was anything to admire—she wanted to be gracious—but her eye encountered only signs of comfort and bad taste; fortunately a dog rushed out of the kitchen, and on this she showered compliments, leaving a pleasant glow. Her curiosity was going to be satisfied, she could get on with Lynch—she liked him—and it was comforting not to have had to write a cheque.

Disquiet set in later. Why had Mr Robinson not told her his real name? It was uncanny to hear Lynch speak of him as Norval. She had heard that name before. An unusual name. It had some unpleasant association. She worried over it and very nearly rang Mr Lynch up; but restrained herself, fearing loss of dignity.

At night, in bed, she remembered. Then she recalled every moment of their association, waking up to see him crouching over her, his hands working so strangely, that time in the motor car when—Miss Kelly screamed aloud.

She was alone in her miniature four-poster, and the Ridleys would have hardly heard her. She turned on the light and listened to the throbbing of her heart.

II

WHEN MISS KELLY had taken her departure—ex-Superintendent Lynch came as far as the gate and waved her away—he took up the telephone and rang the Guards at Swords, and asked to speak to the sergeant in charge; then he went to his writing-desk and pulled out a large file to which he attached the letter he had been given by Miss Kelly. He would have liked to call his wife in to tell her all about it, but he was afraid she might notice his excitement and try to put a stop to the cause of it.

Miss Kelly arrived early the following afternoon bearing gifts of dahlias and jam, sops to Cerberus in the person of Mrs Lynch, who greeted her warmly.

"Daddy, here's Miss Kelly to see you, and she's brought a pot of your favourite jam."

"Daddy" sounded ridiculous to Miss Kelly but otherwise she had nothing to complain at about her reception. A chair was drawn up at a table beside the turf fire in the hearth, and on it lay a fat manuscript, the top sheet blue.

"I happened to be passing," she began, but Mr Lynch put a stop to her overture by putting an arm round her shoulders.

"Sit you down there, and take all the time you want. If you need anything, you've only to call."

Miss Kelly was grateful to be left alone. The homely unpretentious comfort of the room, like its usual occupants, reassured her. Whatever she might discover in her research, she felt safe here. The first part of the file was taken up with official papers, all headed "The State v Nevil Norval", and these, though grim, did not detain her. When she came to a paper headed "Statement of the prisoner to Detective Sergeant Lynch", she pulled the papers closer to her and very soon was lost to any consciousness of time or place. Because the narrative was in the first person, the necessity to reconcile Mr Robinson with someone called Nevil Norval didn't arise, and as she hadn't a visual imagination, she was not troubled by the fact that she was reading the confession of a boy. It would have been impossible to imagine Mr Robinson taking a ride on the pillion of someone's motorcycle, for example.

The prisoner was describing his movements on the day of the crime. "I had gone to bed late and slept very badly. Max Morrison, my room-mate, came home at 1 a.m. He had been out to supper after the theatre. He was in a very angry mood; whoever his supper friends were they told him that my mother had been spreading rumours about him, that he had stolen money and other things from her, including clothes, that he was a pervert and had corrupted me and she had caught us in the act and forbidden me the house until I broke with him completely. Max said I was to tell my mother he was taking proceedings against her for defamation of character. I was staying with him because my parents didn't want me. I was welcome to go as soon as either was prepared to show natural parental instincts. Max said my father could have had my mother up for attempting to poison him, but he refrained for the sake of the family's reputation. I objected to his tone, and he lost his temper and told me to leave the next day. I think he had drunk too much, but it is difficult to tell with him. He locked the door of the bedroom and ordered me to sleep on the sofa. I hoped he would be in a better mood in the morning, but he stayed in his room, and I went over to the theatre with the hope of seeing Maurice Elvery. I decided to mention the tour to him again. If he was prepared to give me a definite engagement in the theatre with a salary after we returned, I thought I might be able to persuade my father to put up the money for the tour.

"When I arrived at the theatre it was twelve o'clock. Maurice had called a rehearsal of the scene in the pawnbroker's room. There had been some difficulty about the axe. He has it concealed on his person, and the old woman when he gives her the parcel to open is not supposed to see it. I watched this: the axe was a fake, of course; but I noticed for the first time that it was exactly the same shape as the one we had at home for chopping up logs. I waited until the lunch-break; Maurice didn't seem to want to talk to me. I decided to call on my father; if I went at once, I'd catch him before he went back to his office. I arrived at Eglinton Terrace at approximately half-past one. He was alone, and invited me to join him. He was having bread and cheese. He said he was distressed by rumours about Max Morrison, that if I was associated with him it would injure my reputation. If I would agree to leave him and give up the theatre, I could live with him and he would try to use his influence to get me into some of the tobacco companies. He was sorry I had shown no taste for the law; but it was hopeless to apprentice myself if my heart wasn't in it. And he agreed that I would never pass the final examination. It is quite stiff.

"He was quite friendly, but when I plucked up courage to ask him to pay my expenses on tour, he said he wouldn't if Max were going. I couldn't shake him. As my mother had approved of my going to the Phoenix, he couldn't see why she was not prepared to put up the money. She could afford it better than he. I left Eglinton Terrace at half-past two. I walked to the station in Ranelagh and took a train to Carrickmines. My mother was not at home. Ellen Toomey, a girl who worked in the house, but lived out, said she thought she was playing golf with Miss Birch. I waited until nearly six. My mother came in then and behaved in a most eccentric manner, pretending not to see me, talking to the maid as if they were alone in the house. I had to be in the theatre half an hour before curtain-up at eight. When Ellen left, I went into the kitchen and shut the door. My mother was preparing a chicken at the table. I told her about the tour and that I had called on my father first. She asked me where I thought she would find the money.

"I said it was only £50. I said I would return it in instalments when I came back. Going on the tour meant that I was becoming a regular member of the company. If I didn't go, I would still be a mere hanger-on. Calling me an 'apprentice' was only a device to avoid paying me for the work I was doing. If I left they would have no difficulty in getting others who would give anything to get the chance of parts.

" 'When we have one Queen's Theatre, I can't see the need for another,' my mother said. I reminded her that she had been keen on my joining the Phoenix originally.

130

" 'I didn't realise it would mean you had to become a bugger to keep your place. That's your father's objection to it, and for once I find myself in agreement with him.'

"I said that was a lie. She said everyone knew about Max; and then I told her that he had heard about her gossiping and was throwing me out. She said that was the best news she had heard in a long time. I asked her if I could stay there. I had nowhere to go. Max said he wouldn't let me back into the flat. I had my things in a suitcase in the theatre. She said that I could sleep in my room, but she wouldn't give me meals. I'd have to look after myself.

"I had to run to catch the train. She didn't offer to drive me. It was lashing rain, and I had only a light coat. I was wet and tired and hungry when I arrived at the theatre at ten minutes to eight, and I had to dress in a hurry.

"When the performance was over I went to Max's dressing-room and asked if I could come back to his flat for the night. I didn't feel like making the journey back to Carrickmines in my wet clothes. He refused. I caught the half-past eleven train from Harcourt Street and walked from there to my mother's house. It was raining heavily. There were no lights on when I arrived, and I supposed she had gone to bed. When I tried to open the door with my latchkey, I found the lock had been changed. I remembered a way that I had got in before by climbing on to the garage roof. The bathroom window was only a few feet above this level, and it was usually unfastened. I got in without any difficulty. I tried the door of my mother's room. It was locked. I decided not to disturb her. My own bed was made. I was shivering and very hungry, and unable to go to sleep. I decided to go down to the kitchen and make myself a hot drink and see if there was a spare hot-water bottle.

"When I was waiting for the kettle to boil, my mother shouted from upstairs, 'Who is it?' I answered. She made no reply, and I assumed she must have gone back to her room. A few minutes later, I heard a shriek and the sound of someone falling downstairs. I went out at once and found my mother at the foot of the stairs; her head was against the pedestal of an oriental bronze lamp in the hall. I turned on the light, until then

131

there was only the light from the kitchen. I saw my mother's head was in a pool of blood. I tried to lift her, but she was very heavy and I could only prop her up against the stairs. I took a towel in the cloakroom and soaked it in water and tried to stay the flow of blood. Her eyes were open and rolled back. I felt her wrists, but I knew she was dead. I telephoned Max and told him what had happened. I asked him to help me; he said it was my own affair. I would have called for the doctor, but I knew he could do nothing. Meanwhile, blood had got everywhere. It was all over my clothes and shoes and there was a pool on the hall carpet and on the stairs. I got a basin and put it under my mother's head. I thought of ringing up my father; but I was afraid he might suspect me of being the cause of my mother's death. I was afraid to call in the Guards for the same reason. My mother changing the lock on the door and locking herself into her room showed her attitude towards me. I could only guess what she might have been saying. I had heard the accusations she made against my father. My friend's refusing to help me was the last straw. After that I felt that I didn't stand a chance. Then I decided to get rid of the body. My mother used to go down to Malahide Island to play golf. She had friends in the neighbourhood. I had fished in the estuary between Swords and Donabate. It was only a few miles away and quite deserted. At this time of night there would be nobody about. I knew one place where I used to tie up my boat. I could run the car into the water and put the body into the sea. My mother always drove herself; I had no licence.

"That was as far as I could organise my thinking. My mother was in her nightdress. I put her fur coat on over it and dragged her through the kitchen and into the garage. I put her into the back of the car. There was no key in the ignition. I had to go back and look for it. My mother's bag was in her room with the key in it. I took the bag and put it in the car. Then I drove very slowly into Dublin and out to Swords by the Belfast road. There was no traffic. I passed three cars on the journey. I was not quite certain of the way to the jetty I was looking for; but I turned off the road to Donabate and followed a sign pointing to a place the name of which I didn't recognise, but it was in the direction I was aiming at. The road narrowed to a lane after passing the entrance to a large house. I recognised the place. I was within fifty yards of the water's edge, and then I saw a van of some kind, without lights, parked on the left in front of me, leaving a narrow gap.

"I stopped the car and got out and went to inspect. A caravan, obviously empty, dumped there by travelling tinkers presumably. It was quite impossible to move it. There were probably other ways to reach the estuary but I was afraid that in my efforts to turn the car I might get stuck in the lane, and of the two risks I decided to try to get past the caravan. I paced the width and there was about six inches to spare. I drove very carefully but the front bumper caught in the wheel of the caravan. I backed to get free and in turning the steering-wheel increased the angle; when I came forward again the left front wheel got caught, and I could neither go back nor forward.

"I had no option but to leave the car where it was and pull my mother into the sea. I climbed into the back of the car to test the door, how far it would open. I had to pull the body up into a sitting position. Before I could open the door, the head-lights of a car blazed through the back window and then switched off. Nobody got out. Whoever was there could see me with their side-lights, which had been left on. I looked back. A match flared and I saw the faces of a young man and a girl. It was half-past one. I put my arm around my mother's shoulders. To the couple behind us, we looked like lovers. I sat like that for an hour, then the engine of the car behind started up and the full lights came on. I opened the rear window although it was pouring rain outside in case the driver might ask me a question. However, he backed up the lane and turned into the sweep at the entrance to the big house. When the car had gone, I tried the door and found that I had enough space to get myself out. I pulled the body towards the door and tried to lift it, but I was stiff and cold and she seemed the weight of lead. I had to pull it along the ground. It was so wet and dark that I was tempted to turn on the headlights, but decided the risk was too great if anyone were to turn up now.

"When my eyes grew accustomed to the dark, I could make out the jetty, a shadow on the sea. I stepped down on to gravel,

133

and walked for a few yards before I felt my shoes in water. The tide must have been full in. The jetty consisted of a few planks, and I nearly fell off it several times. When I got to the end, I let the body slide into the water. I went back to the car and made one last effort to move it. The caravan was well bogged down as if it had been standing there since summer. I knew there was a path round the edge of the estuary, but it was too difficult to negotiate in this weather at night. I walked back the way I came. It was half-past three when I reached the Dublin road.

"I walked as far as Swords, and there I signalled a passing motorist who stopped and I asked him if he would give me a lift to Dublin. He refused, drove on, and then thought better of it and halted. When I came up he asked me where I was going and I said 'Foxrock'. He said he was going to Bray and he would drop me at the Foxrock road. At first he seemed suspicious of me and he must have seen I was wet up to the knees; but I said I had to abandon my car and that I had been working on my boat. He then talked freely, and insisted on driving me home. I gave him the wrong address as I did not want him to recognise it afterwards. I had about a mile and a half to walk from there. I took a bath when I got home, and I then lay down and slept. When I woke up it was daylight. I went downstairs. There was blood all over the lower steps of the stair carpet and on the hall parquet. I tried to wash it out, but when I couldn't, I cut the carpet away and put the stained piece into the stove. There was blood all over my clothes and shoes. The telephone rang twice, but I didn't answer it. I put all the clothes I was wearing and the shoes into a box. Ellen Toomey came after lunch. I asked her if my mother said anything to her about going away because I hadn't seen her since yesterday. Ellen said she was talking to my mother in the afternoon and she said nothing about going away, and told her to lay one place for dinner and roast a chicken.

"I told her I had cut my hand badly and spilt blood on the carpet. I had in fact cut my hand at the jetty, and the man driving me into Dublin noticed it. Ellen asked if I had telephoned any of my mother's friends for information. I said I had not. Later in the afternoon, two Guards called; they said my mother's car had been found abandoned near Swords. I told them I had not seen her since yesterday and I had been in the theatre in the evening. I had to go into Dublin for that evening's performance. The Guards drove me into Dublin and one of them asked me what was the matter with my hand. I said I had cut it on glass. After the performance, I asked Max Morrison to let me return to the flat, but he refused. I went back to Carrickmines by the last train."

This statement was signed "Nevil Norval"; it was a typewritten copy, and there was no handwriting.

"Have you found out what you want to know?"

The voice of the former detective came to Miss Kelly from somewhere outside space. Without looking up, she said, "He didn't do it, then."

"You've been reading his statement."

"Yes."

"He didn't give evidence at the trial. His lawyers decided not to put him into the witness-box."

"Why?"

"They must have considered he wouldn't stand up to cross-examination."

"And do you mean to say that in spite of that statement, he was still found guilty?"

"Yes. The judge instructed the jury that they might accept the evidence of death, but added that they were under no obligation to accept the rest of the statement."

"How monstrously unfair. How could they take the bit that suited them and then reject the rest?"

"They acted in the light of all the evidence. There was blood all over the place. Mrs Norval's clothes were in her room. She was unlikely to go driving at night in a nightdress and fur coat. And an axe in the woodshed had blood on the blade. Very little, admittedly; the merest speck, but then an axe blow doesn't usually leave much blood on the blade."

"Someone sharpening the blade might have cut himself."

"Certainly. Then there was the behaviour of the prisoner. He finds his mother missing and yet he doesn't even ring up to enquire. When the Guards called, he showed very little concern."

"And how do you know?"

"I was one of them."

"And did you not believe his statement?"

"I tried to keep an open mind, as I always did; it was the only way to do our job efficiently. You must be impersonal, and just weigh the facts. What weighed against Norval from the start was his anxiety, not on his mother's account, but to conceal evidence against himself, burning the stained carpet, for example."

"And what about this Max person, was he investigated? What did he have to say at the trial?"

"Very little. He corroborated Norval's statement. There was a telephone call put through to him that night. He told the court—it's in the transcript there—that Norval wasn't paying his share of the rent and that he had taken him in only for kindness, and when his father offered to find him a flat, he insisted on Nevil's taking the offer. It all hung together. He didn't make a good impression. As you probably know, he was in trouble on a few occasions over cheques. But he had no hand in the murder; and his only concern was to have nothing to do with Norval once he heard he was in trouble."

Miss Kelly hid her face in her hands; what shocked her was not the possibility that Mr Robinson had murdered his mother but that she was not revolted by the possibility. She would help him to establish his innocence; but if he was not innocent? He was. He was. He must be. Otherwise she couldn't live with herself. Max was the one.

Mr Lynch took the file off the table, moving gently.

"I think you've read quite enough for one day," he said. "Would you ever take an old man's advice, who only wishes you well?"

"What is it?" Miss Kelly always bridled when she was asked to agree to any proposition in advance.

"Don't bother your head any more with this business. It isn't the sort of thing I'd get myself mixed up with, if I were you. These were unhappy, sick people, who couldn't make a go of their own lives: most of them are dead, and Mr Robinson is not a gentleman you should be friends with. People don't change; I got to know him very well. Poor fellow, he had to confide in someone. He chose me. He called me 'the examining magistrate'. I think that was some idea he got out of the play you were talking about. I saw a great deal of him. The statement you have just read was given to me in Bewley's, the coffee shop. I took him out to get him away from the atmosphere of crime and detection. I hadn't to lead him. I couldn't stop him talking. Of course, he was putting a rope round his neck; but even so, he couldn't have died without taking someone into his confidence. He would have liked, best of all, to tell his father, if he thought he could have had his father's respect or even affection. He wanted to be a hero. He wanted an audience; and I was prepared to listen all day. It was my job. What does your Mr Robinson want? Even if I were to give him his file he can't blot out the record. If he wants to prove that he didn't kill his mother, none of us can help him."

Miss Kelly stood up, her mouth slightly open, the light of recognition illuminating her eyes.

"He spoke of a girl—he believed that some Sonia of his imagining went to Siberia—the lunatic asylum—with him. There wasn't anyone; there couldn't have been—he is still trying to work it out, to find out what was true. He thought I was his mother and another time—"

But Miss Kelly, suddenly aware of scrutiny, cut off. She had very nearly told this examining magistrate more than she intended to tell anyone.

"Did Mr Robinson tell you about the girl?"

"Which girl?"

"The one who haunted him from the first day of the trial, sat bewitched, couldn't take her eyes off him, wrote passionate love-letters, sent him presents, and tried to organise his escape from the asylum. Storey, I think her name was, Ruth Storey. She gave a great deal of trouble, and was very lucky she didn't find herself in prison. Her father undertook to send her out of the country. I don't know what happened to her afterwards. I often wondered if they met again. It was an extraordinary case of morbid fascination."

"He did say something, now that you mention it, about that girl, but she didn't mean anything to him. I'm sure of that. There was no Sonia for Mr Robinson. He has had years of loneliness, in the most appalling disgrace, because at the time people didn't know as much as they do nowadays. He ought to have had psychiatric treatment. He was the victim of his parents and his upbringing and his evil, so-called friend. He needs help now, and I think it is simply unchristian not to give it to him if we can."

Miss Kelly had found her own voice again. She had been at sea, but now she was back on land, and in the ascendant again. Nobody told Miss Kelly what to do. She asked for advice when she required it, and was accustomed to pay. She gave it, wherever she thought it was needed, for nothing.

Mr Lynch slightly sharpened his tone.

"I don't think either of us is in a position to help Nevil Norval, if he needs help, and, indeed, he may."

"I can't, I know, beyond showing him friendship. He doesn't seem to have any friends. But you are in a better position than anyone to give him peace of mind. Even if there is another copy of the file, all he has asked is that this one should be destroyed."

"This file is not my property, Miss Kelly."

"Then why is it in your house?"

"I was working on it. I should have given it back years ago. I told you this when I said I'd let you look at it. Now, I'm rather sorry I did, but when you have seen as much of it as you need for your purpose, I'll drive into town and leave it where it belongs. I can't see how getting it into his possession is going to help Norval in any way. It's rather late in the day for him to be covering up his tracks; and he must know everything that's on the record. He should leave it alone. And you, if you are a wise woman, will leave him alone."

"I think I've reached the age when I can look after myself, thank you."

"I want you to face the facts. Even then, once he knew his fate was decided and he wasn't going to hang; he wasn't even going to prison, but to a mental hospital—"

"Which was worse."

138

"I don't know. In the circumstances, it wasn't. That's beside the point. What I wanted to say was that once he knew the verdict couldn't be changed, his first impulse was to convince me that he had killed his mother. He couldn't bear that I shouldn't give him credit. I remember well the look on his face, the childish pride. He was determined to impress me. Throughout the trial, he showed no emotion at all. Except once. He looked sad when he confronted his father in court. I must admit that. Indeed, I often wonder how much his father knew. His evidence was strongly weighted in the boy's favour. If one thing more than another persuaded the jury to be lenient, it was that. You should read the father's evidence if you want to get a true picture of the trial. And then, if I were you, I'd go away on a holiday as if you were convalescing after an illness; and put this ugly old nightmare out of your mind."

"May I take the file with me when I'm going?"

"No, Miss Kelly; but you may come back and read it whenever you please."

III

THE EX-SUPERINTENDENT and his wife had a bet. He said that their visitor's pride—she left with great haughtiness, having been refused the file—would prevent her from returning. This bet was laid at their evening meal on the day Miss Kelly called; on the following morning, at eleven o'clock, Mrs Lynch answered a knock at the door; Miss Kelly was standing on the threshold.

"Good morning—is Mr Lynch at home? I just happened to be passing—"

"Come in. Daddy: Miss Kelly to see you."

Mr Lynch came out of his study, and as he showed Miss Kelly in, searched in his pocket, produced a fifty-pence piece and laid it on the hall table.

Miss Kelly turned and faced him. She looked old, he thought. She was rather heavily made up.

"I really don't know what has me here; but you said that I ought to read the evidence of the father in the case, and as I happened to be passing—"

"By all means. You don't have to apologise. I'm at your service. Give me a moment. I used to know this file backwards. Here it is. I think you can read more comfortably at the table. I shall be around the house if you want me."

Miss Kelly was grateful to be left alone. She felt deeply ashamed, as if she had stripped herself in front of this policeman, this stranger, who had advised her for her own good, treating her like a child. And to think that wife of his—a perfectly decent woman in her own way, no doubt—probably knew all about it—was very hurtful to her pride. If she could, she would have stayed away. She had tried numerous expedients, ringing up friends, making appointments—but all to no purpose. This must be what priests call "an occasion of sin", she decided. Never, certainly, had she found any call of duty so irresistible.

She settled her skirt, and with one hand clawing the collar of her turtle-necked jumper, began where the page lay open.

She was disappointed to find no description of Mr Robinson's father beyond the fact of his address and that he was in practice as a solicitor and the prisoner was his son. Not even his age was given nor any clue to his appearance. He must at the time have been about Mr Robinson's age. But did he look like him? However, she was soon lost in the barrister's questions to him and his answers.

He had married in 1917, and his wife, Kathleen Anne, had one child, the prisoner. Their marriage had been difficult from the start, his wife's nervous health was poor; she was advised not to have any more children; after the birth of Nevil her manner and behaviour towards him (her husband) had deteriorated until it developed into a form of persecution. She interrupted his business by perpetual telephoning about trifles, and became abusive when he complained. He discovered that she was calling on his clients and making complaints about his treatment of her: after an incident which he preferred not to go into, they agreed to separate. He took the boy because he did not consider his wife was a suitable person to look after a child. The mother had access to her son at all times, but showed very little interest in him. She led quite a busy social life—she had some private means as well as what he allowed her—and she was popular among her friends.

Nevil was sent to a preparatory school; his reports were poor. He had no aptitude for work, but was reasonably good at games. The headmaster, when he was thirteen, suggested that he be removed from school and given private tuition if he were to stand any chance of passing the entrance to a public school. A tutor was found for him; and it was at this time that he swallowed the sleeping-pills which he found in his father's dressing-room. Fortunately, he was discovered almost at once, and rushed to hospital where a stomach pump was used effectively. He was not a violent boy, but inclined to be morose. He got on well with boys of his own age without making friends. After the attempt to kill himself, he was put under psychiatric care. One of the doctors found him deficient in a sense of responsibility and awareness of other people and their feelings. The other thought that he was simply suffering from the effect of a divided family, and recommended that he should see more of his mother. An arrangement was made by which he slept in his father's house and called on his mother for meals. It was not satisfactory. Later he spent more time with his mother; but she was constantly abusing him. She disliked spending any money on him and referred all bills to his father.

Counsel for the Prosecution asked: When had he last seen his wife?

"One evening about a fortnight before her disappearance."

"How did she seem then?"

"Very nervous and excitable; she had taken exception to Nevil's manner of life and associates. She said she would not allow him to stay in her house. As a result of this conversation, I called on Nevil and offered to pay for a furnished flat for him."

"And what had he said to that?"

"He said he would prefer to stay where he was."

"Was that the last time you saw the prisoner?"

"It was."

"Did he make any reference to his mother?"

"He regretted her attitude. There was nothing violent or vindictive in his manner. He had never stood up to his mother or attempted to return her abuse. She could be very abusive. He (Mr Norval) did not consider that she was wholly sane. She had often threatened to take her own life. He had taken medical advice about it, but agreed with the doctors that her extreme behaviour was confined to her family, and the prospect was better for her if she separated from them."

Miss Kelly read on: Why was there no reference to Max Morrison or the scene in Mrs Norval's bedroom? These were vital. *Where was that man?* She had her finger on the bell, but restrained herself in time, opened the door and saw, at the end of the passage, Mr Lynch inserting a screw in a wall. He saw her and came at once.

"Is that *all*?" she said, pointing at the file, majestic now.

142

"Of the father's evidence you mean?"

"You said it was all there."

"That's an exact transcript."

"But you saw Mr Robinson's letter. You read his statement. Why did the father not tell about the time when Max made him put on his mother's clothes and the awful way Max spoke to the mother?"

"It wasn't calculated to win the sympathy of the jury, was it? But, in any event, the father could only give evidence of what he himself had seen and heard, not a second-hand account. That's hearsay evidence."

"And you call that a fair trial?" Miss Kelly was trembling.

"If there had been any evidence to connect Max Morrison with Mrs Norval's death, then he would have been charged. But there wasn't. Nevil was insistent that Max refused to be associated with his actions on that day. And you are not going to suggest that Max did the killing on his own; he was in the theatre on that evening in a leading part.

"You have interested yourself in this Mr Robinson of yours, and you are indignant to see what he has had to suffer when a really nasty little fellow like Max can live comfortably off susceptible old women; but that's life, I'm afraid."

Miss Kelly did not like anyone thwarting her; but she was impressed by firm men. The case was clearly hopeless, and she would have to report to Mr Robinson exactly what had occurred and let him know that she had done all she could. There was one hope remaining, if this nice man (for such she deemed him) could be persuaded to see Mr Robinson, if only once, that might be sufficient to put his mind at rest. When he knew that there was positively no hope of altering the record, then he might concentrate on the future, and, for what it was worth, if it meant anything to him—he would have her assurance that she believed in his innocence.

Mr Lynch was intelligent and experienced, but a man with his background could not possibly appreciate the sophistication of the *Crime and Punishment* angle. He seemed to attach no importance to the fact that Nevil Norval, at the most impressionable age, under the influence of a corrupt and clever friend, in a most

143

peculiar relation to his mother, was subconsciously undergoing an extraordinary therapy. She was not in the least a literary person, but she was accustomed to the society of people like Cyril Forbes, who would only have met Mr Lynch in the event of a burglary. He could not be expected to see the matter in other than a pedestrian point of view. He was obviously full of common sense and she rather liked his lapses into plain speaking, because he never forgot his place. She forgot hers when he rigidly resisted her request that he would give Mr Robinson an interview. She was haughty and tearful by turns.

"Why can't you? What harm could it possibly do?"

"I haven't many years to go, Miss Kelly, and the best part of my life was given to crime. I did my duty. I'm entitled to a few years when I can call my soul my own. If Nevil Norval was on my conscience, if I had stepped outside my duty to hurt him in any way, I'd make any reparation I could; but I didn't. And I believe he was tried fairly and convicted justly. I don't know whether he was mad or not; but I find it hard to believe—as the jury found it hard to believe—that anybody who was sane could kill his own mother. I'll admit I was curious when he cropped up again, but I'm not going to reopen that horrible case. I am going to forget Nevil Norval after today and I'd advise you to forget Mr Robinson."

Dermot Lynch had considerable strength of mind; it accounted to some extent for his remarkable state of preservation at seventy-five. He did succeed in dismissing the Norval case from his mind, from the day after Miss Kelly's departure with scorn on her lips and tears in her eyes.

She, not the protagonist of the drama, was the subject of discussion at his evening meal that day. "God forgive me for saying so, but a roll in the ditch with one of my lads when she was the right age for it, would have spared her all this," he reflected aloud.

"I'd like to see her face if she heard you," his wife remarked. "Eat up; your food's getting cold."

A few days passed; Miss Kelly had not telephoned or called; Mr Lynch was reading his newspaper, when he got up suddenly and announced that he was going into Dublin.

"What has come over you all of a sudden?" his wife enquired. He handed her the newspaper and pointed to a paragraph which read:

Mr Max Morrison

Mr Max Morrison, who was found dead in his residence, The Maltings, Ashwell, Herts, on Monday last, was formerly a well-known figure in the art world of Dublin, and acted for two seasons at the Phoenix Theatre under Maurice Elvery's management. Born in Gowran, Co. Kilkenny in 1905, Mr Morrison lived in England since his retirement from the stage. He was a prominent rosegrower and won many medals. At the time of his death, he was living alone. His body was discovered after he had been dead for some days. A coroner's inquest returned a verdict of death from natural causes. Dr Robert Perry, who had been attending the deceased, said his heart was affected and he had recently advised him to avoid any undue exertion or unnecessary excitement. The Irish Ambassador was represented at the funeral which took place at Golder's Green Crematorium yesterday.

IV

MISS KELLY'S FRIENDS were anxious about her. She played, it must be admitted, no very vital rôle in their lives. None, were it to please God to call her to Him, would have lost an hour's sleep in consequence, but she had become an institution. To Aggie, for instance, she represented wealth and ease, and it satisfied some need in Mrs Fitzsimons' nature to act as part-time lady-in-waiting. Cyril Forbes, and, to a lesser extent, Eric Phipps and George Warren, liked to go to her lunches and dinners because she accepted them as non-marrying men; she did not economise over food or wine, and she was not encumbered with a family. There was nobody at Miss Kelly's except Miss Kelly; no enquiries had to be made about the health or progress of anybody else. The women in her immediate circle, Mrs Knox Knox, Lady Jamieson and the rest, were either widowed or from some other cause unattached; and there was a nice pattern-making for parties; after married couples had been thrown in with abandon, it was necessary to discover how many of the dear queers were free for the occasion before calling on the pool of always available women. This was all done in an open, no-nonsense fashion. As each knew every move of the other, it was a rule of the game to give details to the uninvited, whetting appetite. And so the ball was kept rolling.

Miss Kelly's friends were worried because she had suddenly given up the game. When it came to her turn, she let the opportunity pass; she pleaded unconvincing excuses for refusing to come out. Everyone knew about the romance; if telephones were tapped in Ireland the Minister for Posts and Telegraphs would have had a fat file on Mr Robinson. Not all in the Kelly circle were familiar with the Irish past; some had come to Ireland to live for various reasons, none of them sound, and stayed on from inertia. Mabel Ormsby, the least ornamental of the group, never able to hold her own when conversation got off the ground, tasted glory unexpectedly at this critical time. She had "come out" in the same year as Miss Kelly, and had settled for the first offer, sacrificing her nubility on an altar which Miss Kelly would have despised. But she seemed content in her suburb and was forever bringing up topics from the past. A cheerful little body, in her post-prandial telephone conversation circuit she alluded to the death of Max Morrison as someone she remembered at parties, who had disappeared, whom she had heard rather doubtful accounts of. She rang no bell among the comparative newcomers (twenty-five years' residence, say), but Cyril Forbes knew exactly about whom she was talking.

"A nasty bit of work," he said, and added some detail which unloosed further reminiscence from Mrs Ormsby. "Wasn't he connected in some way with that awful Norval case, the boy who murdered his mother and dropped her in the sea?"

"They shared a flat," Cyril informed her, and now because Max was dead and life was rather boring and he had absolutely nothing to do and was comfortably propped up on pillows in bed and had finished breakfast, he embarked on a long delicious gossip about the topic of the hour.

"Do you know who Mr Robinson that none of us is allowed to meet is?"

(Aggie Fitzsimons was not in the circle. She inhabited outer social space.)

"No. Tell me."

"Norval, Nevil Norval."

"Does she know?"

"I can't tell. She is so very peculiar these days. But I think she must because she is always at such pains not to let me know anything, and, of course, can't keep it up. As soon as she told me he had shared a flat with Max Morrison I knew at once."

"But can you believe it?"

"I heard he had gone abroad somewhere. I must say, if I were he, I shouldn't want ever to see Ireland again; but I suppose it might have a morbid fascination; they say the murderer is drawn back to the scene of the crime. I don't know, not having committed a murder as yet, except in my mind, which reeks with unburied corpses."

147

"But this is very frightening. Or at least it frightens me. Don't you think you ought to warn her. She isn't herself, poor dear. He has done something to her. Upset her, I mean."

"Wouldn't you be upset if you fell for a dark, if elderly, stranger and discovered too late that he had dispatched his mother with an axe? I should."

"Cyril, you are awful. This isn't a joking matter. I do think we ought to try to help. I don't suppose there's any actual danger, do you? I mean, if he was going to bump someone else off, he'd have done it long ago? Everyone at the time said his mother was pretty terrible, or so I seem to remember."

"The story was that she treated him like dirt. Nobody was particularly sorry for her. There was even an effort to rescue him. I heard that some of his theatre friends helped to organise it. So they must have sympathised. Although, I must say—"

"Quite. And there was some girl, don't you remember, who haunted the trial, and was clearly infatuated. I heard that it was she who was responsible for the rescue attempt. I wonder what happened to *her*. I can't even remember her name, can you?"

"No. It was nobody we knew. She must have been barmy. But, you see, the fact that he had axed his mother only turned her on. It can happen."

"Cyril! You don't mean to suggest that—"

"I don't know what to say; but she is in a wretched state, and I would be glad to hear that Mr Robinson had returned to Australia or wherever."

"Do you think I could help by talking to her? She has no one to talk to."

"There's that Aggie Fitzsimons to whom she is so mysteriously attached. I can never understand the bond. I should think she is a recipient of every confidence. I've met her a few times. She's very motherly and put-downable. I should say she has had a blow-by-blow account. I must confess, if it weren't for all the gory mess, I'd be glad that at last something had *happened* to our dear friend. I always said that nothing but a stick of dynamite would ever shake her; and it seems that Mr Robinson has managed to produce it. Well, after all, Queen Victoria had to go through it."

"Cyril, you are not suggesting—really, you are impossible. You won't take anything seriously; and this is serious, or it might be. These are the times one needs one's friends."

"Well, my dear, if there's anything you think I can do, tell me. We must all try to keep in touch with her, not allow her to go into herself too much. But I asked her to come here for the weekend and she refused. In the past, she always jumped at it. Mr Robinson may take himself off now; that's the best we can hope for. I don't think he would make a suitable *parti*."

Miss Kelly was the only subject discussed by her friends when Cyril Forbes broke his silence about Max.

She was afraid to go out in case Mr Robinson should telephone or call and she might miss him. She believed that he would go away now, but not without an enquiry as to how she had got on with his "examining magistrate". She had stopped asking herself whether he was innocent or guilty. It had ceased to matter. She only wanted to serve him and be the friend he never had. His was the saddest story she had ever heard. Everything against him, and not even religion to give him some support. No parents, no friends. Instead, a mad mother, and a bad friend.

She knew her little circle were concerned about her, and she was embarrassed at the thought of how much she had given herself away. None of them, *as men*, could compare with Mr Lynch. If she had married a man like that, she could have adapted him to her ways very easily. A woman was different; that sort of man was always handicapped by an impossible wife. Pity. She smiled at herself, remembering a time when she told a friend that she would never be able to face the intimacies of marriage with a man who pronounced H "haitch".

She was alone on the afternoon the telephone rang; her heart leaped; she couldn't for a moment breathe, then, shaking herself, she picked up the receiver.

"Is that Miss Kelly?" It was not *his* voice. Her own hardened at once. "Who is that?"

"This is Dermot Lynch speaking, Miss Kelly. I shouldn't be

surprised if Mr Robinson were to call on you in the near future. If he does, I want you to let me know. I shouldn't ask if it weren't serious. I think you know that."

"You said you never wanted to hear of the case again. That was your excuse for refusing to see Mr Robinson."

"I know, but circumstances have changed."

"What circumstances, may I ask?"

"Max Morrison was found dead in the hallway of his house a few days ago."

"I don't see what that has to do with Mr Robinson."

"Morrison lived in Ashwell in Hertfordshire; Mr Robinson spent the night previous in the Cromwell Hotel in Stevenage. Hertfordshire is a small county, Miss Kelly. And I find the coincidence alarming."

"There are thousands of Robinsons in the world."

"Certainly, but not with addresses in Perth, Western Australia."

"Are you making an accusation against Mr Robinson? Is this coincidence to be used as a new excuse for persecuting him? What did Max die of?"

"Heart failure. He had a bad heart. But the doctor said he looked a badly frightened man."

"Pain in the heart is frightful. I saw my brother once."

"Quite so. I am ringing up because I am worried about you. For no other reason. Will you make me that promise?"

"If you promise to see Mr Robinson."

"I agree to that."

"You promise?"

"I promise."

"Goodbye, Mr Lynch."

"Goodbye, Miss Kelly."

She was smiling with gratification as she put down the receiver. Nice and kind as she had found the policeman, she had never been able to have her own way with him before. She would write at once to Mr Robinson; but she didn't know his address. How provoking! "Damn," she said to herself aloud, before she turned away from the telephone.

Mr Robinson was standing in the doorway. She tried to

speak, but could say nothing. She had to sit down to recover her breath; her heart was beating violently.

"Where—where—have—you—come—from?" she got out at last, through painful breaths, and pointed to a chair.

"The door was open. You must forgive me."

Miss Kelly put her hand to her chest; she was really incapable of speaking. She could take in his appearance now. He was his usual meticulously dressed self. Like a bank manager. It was impossible to imagine him on a ranch.

She smiled at him reassuringly. Soon, she seemed to say, she would be in a condition to talk to him. She recalled her telephone conversation. How much had he heard? Her eyes travelled in the direction of the instrument, and when they came back, met his, which had made the same journey.

When she could speak, the first thing she said was that she had been speaking to Lynch.

"And what had he to say for himself? Why did he refuse to see me?"

"He was ill when you came over here last, and he is old and wants to forget the past, or so he says. But now he will see you. He took a great deal of persuading. I've called on him twice. He promised. And I don't think he would ever go back on a promise."

Mr Robinson gave no sign of pleasure. His eyes never left Miss Kelly's face. They were slightly reproachful, like a jealous husband's who has no evidence but a nose for atmosphere. When he was away, she forgot what a difficult person he was to please, and how easy to annoy.

"I'll ask Mrs Ridley to bring us tea."

"Not for me, thank you."

"I always have some at this time, unless you'd like something stronger after your journey."

"Tea will do very well."

Miss Kelly went out, and Mr Robinson listened to her giving instructions; all doors were open. When Miss Kelly came back, she had recovered and she attempted to control the situation.

"Tell me, first of all, where are you staying, and what are your

151

plans? I wondered if it might be wise to strike while the iron is hot and invite Mr Lynch to call over. If I were to ask him to come to dinner—would he want to bring Mrs Lynch? Well, it can't be helped. I'll talk to her—what do you say?"

Miss Kelly was asking a great many questions and not waiting for Mr Robinson to answer one of them; but that was partly from nervousness; he would not relax his stare. How much of her telephone conversation had he heard? If only he would agree to her telephoning Lynch, then she would have nothing on her conscience. She wished now that she hadn't given her promise to Lynch: but she hadn't promised to report at once, there was no stipulation about that.

"Have you your bag with you? Did you come by car?" Anything to get that reproachful look off Mr Robinson's face.

"I hired a car in England. I came over by the ferry."

"Why didn't you call me?"

Mr Robinson didn't answer; his eyes seemed to be saying "How could you have done this to me?" But what had she done? Made herself a laughing stock among her friends on his account, pestered this decent Lynch man on his account, immersed herself in the most loathsome details of his trial, concentrated on him to the exclusion of everything else; and if she had made a promise to Lynch, it was only to prevent him from taking action. If he was so suspicious of Mr Robinson, he would have alerted the local Guards, had probably done so in any case, because—and when she remembered the reason for his call, Mr Robinson's reproachful behaviour became quite intolerable—he suspected him of having been responsible for Max Morrison's death. That was how a policeman's mind worked, understandably. Crime and suspicion were the nature of his business, and certainly Mr Robinson's behaviour supported a sinister interpretation. The woman in her, she told herself, understood. She had never identified herself to anything like the same extent with anyone in her life before—Michael was always above and beyond her, never close. It was extraordinary how nothing deflected her; the most shocking circumstances which, in the ordinary course of life, she would have refused to listen to—would have put her off anyone who even recounted

152

them—were accepted and excused. She had made her mind into a washing machine so far as Mr Robinson was concerned. Nothing was examined until it had undergone that purifying process. He had a nerve to sulk like this.

"What have I done?" she demanded.

"Done? I don't know what you have done, Miss Kelly. I was not here."

"I know that. I had your letter, but you didn't leave me any address, and I couldn't write to you. I called on Mr Lynch. He was very nice to me, but he refused to part with the file, said it was not his. I tried to talk him round, but he is a very determined man. However, he let me read it. When you came in just now, I had got him to promise to see you."

"Had he refused before?"

"Yes. I couldn't get him to budge."

"And what inducement did you offer him to change his mind right now?"

"Inducement?"

"Yes. Did he ring you up, or you him?"

"Does it matter?"

"I think so."

"Let me see; he rang me up."

"Why?"

"He wanted to know if I had seen you."

"But you told me, he refused to take any interest in me. It bothered his old age."

"He wanted to tell me that Max Morrison was dead."

"And why should he want to tell *you* that?"

"I'll tell you why. When I read about the trial, I was very indignant because Max had been let off so easily. He had been such a bad friend to you, such a downright evil sort of person, setting you against your mother, apart from the fact that he was obviously an undesirable associate for any young man. What disgusted me finally—I'd have forgiven the rest—was his refusal to help you when you rang up and told him you had discovered your mother's dead body. If anything proved your innocence, it was that. Who would murder his mother, and then ring up an inveterate gossip to give him the news? I wish I had been your lawyer. You were very badly served by whoever was retained for you."

Miss Kelly, having wandered off her line, couldn't remember in what direction she had been going, except, vaguely, as far as possible away from the former detective.

"And what had Lynch to say about Max Morrison's death?"

"Just that he had read an account of it in an English newspaper."

"That was all?"

"I think so. He said there was an inquest. The body had been found alone in the house he was living in, somewhere in Hertfordshire."

"Did he ask you for anything in return for this interesting piece of information?"

"Of course not. Why should he? What a ridiculous idea!"

"Are you sure?"

"Certain, of course."

"Then, may I ask, what you promised Mr Lynch?"

"*Promised*?"

"Come on now, Miss Kelly. I heard you. There was an exchange of promises. What were they?"

"Well, if you must know, he asked me to promise I'd let him know if you turned up again; and I used that as an opportunity to get him to promise he'd see you. I was rather pleased with myself, to tell you the truth."

"Pleased with yourself? For promising to betray me? Judas hanged himself."

"Well, you do fancy yourself, I must say. What a comparison! Naturally they are suspicious if in fact you called on Max Morrison. Did you?"

"Why should I tell you?"

"Did you?"

"And if I say I did, you will ring up and report it as soon as my back is turned. What sort of a fool do you take me for?"

"I don't take you for a fool. I think you are the most ungrateful, suspicious person I've ever met. What have I been doing ever since you wrote to me but trying to carry out your wishes. Do you believe it was easy for me? I can't understand my own behaviour. And then you behave as if I was in a conspiracy against you; it's more than anyone could bear."

Miss Kelly was crying. Mr Robinson left his chair, and came beside her on the sofa.

"Stop crying," he said. She stopped.

"Now listen to me. I am not ungrateful. But I happen to have overheard most of your recent telephone conversation. I wasn't eavesdropping. I was in full view; but you kept your back turned, and I didn't interrupt you. I have had my life ruined by the cunning and stupidity of the Irish police; I'm not going to walk into the same trap twice. I want you to tell me, word for word, what Lynch said to you."

Miss Kelly repeated the telephone conversation. When she had finished, Mr Robinson said, "Now what I want you to promise *me* is that you will on no account speak to Lynch or to any other policeman on the telephone unless I am present."

"But how can I say when I may get a call? I think that's unreasonable. I shall certainly promise to tell you exactly what is said if Mr Lynch rings me up."

"Miss Kelly, I shan't be here very long. I am not going to have telephone conversations about me taking place when my back is turned. Lynch will be on the telephone this evening probably. If you don't promise, I shall cut the wires."

"You'll do nothing of the sort. This is my house, Mr Robinson. If you want help, I'll put you in touch with Mr Maxwell, who looked after Michael's affairs, and who advises me whenever I need a solicitor, which isn't often. The firm has always acted for our family; and I'm certain they will take up the matter with the Guards for you. And what they say will be respected; but if you start cutting telephone wires, what's anyone to think? I've never heard of anything like it."

"You don't know what these people are like, Miss Kelly. You don't know about anything outside your doll's house existence. And I'd ask you not to tell me how to manage my own business. I'll manage it as I've always managed it, with no help from anyone. Now, I want that promise."

"What am I to say if Mr Lynch rings me up?"

"If I'm in, it doesn't matter, talk away. If I'm not—but that's

155

not what we are talking about: what I want you to promise is that you won't go ringing him up behind my back."

"You shouldn't ask me to promise any such thing. It's insulting. But if it gives you any peace of mind, I will."

At this point, Mrs Ridley came in with the tea tray.

"Where does *she* sleep?" Mr Robinson enquired when she had left the room.

"The Ridleys have a suite of rooms in the wing, quite cut off from me. Why?"

"Did you mention my name to them?"

"Not today. But they must know who you are. They haven't any friends locally. What are you afraid of?"

"I'm not afraid, Miss Kelly. I don't care for gossiping tongues, that's all."

"Where are you staying tonight? Would you like to stay here?"

"If you could put me up for the night, I'd be very grateful; but I can easily stay in Malahide or at the airport."

"Where's your car?"

"I took the liberty of driving it into the yard. I didn't want to leave it in front of the house. I'll go and fetch my bag."

"There's no need to. The Ridleys will look after it. I'll tell Mrs Ridley you are staying. I'm so glad. I was dining all alone, and I had been given a present of a brace of pheasant. It seemed such a waste."

Miss Kelly had been perfunctory about her toilet recently. Certain rules learned in childhood—the necessity to sponge the face in *cold* water every morning, for example—she obeyed automatically; but she often wore the same clothes for days on end, unable to look further than the chair in her room when she got up in the morning. This evening, she took loving care, bathing herself, and putting on underclothes that she had bought in Paris because they looked so attractive, and had never been worn. She remembered them now. Her frock was a problem. She must look her best and yet not appear to have dressed up or Mrs Ridley would stare, and make her feel self-conscious; in the end she settled for a black silk dress. Nothing she had suited her so well; and its merits were so subtle Mrs Ridley

156

would only notice that she was looking her best. **Mr Robinson,** she hoped, might think so too. At dinner she was the complete hostess, behaving as if she were entertaining the entire diplomatic corps. She looked after the wine herself this time, providing too much.

Mr Robinson ate purposefully and drank sufficiently, answering questions but not initiating conversation. Miss Kelly was satisfied that she was doing all she could to please, and she had determined beforehand not to let the conversation get into its usual rut. After dinner, when he was relaxed, would be time enough to discuss what seemed to be his last objective—a talk with Mr Lynch. Beyond that she had deliberately thought of nothing. For days she had been living with no hope of ever seeing Mr Robinson again; she had him to herself this evening. Nothing done or underdone by her was going to spoil it. On that she had determined, and that, for the present, was enough.

They were in the library where Mrs Ridley had left coffee and the brandy—a wonderful brandy, Cyril had assured her more than once, not that he was often given it—when Miss Kelly introduced the dangerous subject. She had planned to do so and dictate the atmosphere, at the moment she thought appropriate. And now was the moment, for she had run out of conversation.

"I have been wondering about Mr Lynch, how best to arrange for you to see him; why not ring him up now yourself and say you are here? Otherwise, if I don't tell him, he will make that an excuse for not seeing you. He only promised me when I promised him."

"And you know what will happen if I do that?"

"No. How could I?"

"A squad car would call within a quarter of an hour."

"But why? I wish you'd explain."

"You saw yourself what happened as soon as Lynch heard about Max Morrison's death. You can take it from me he was in touch with the detective division at once, and they will be co-operating with Scotland Yard."

"But why? The inquest is over. Death was from natural causes. The fact that you were in Hertfordshire at the time is a

157

coincidence, but you can't be charged on that account. Not in England, certainly."

"I told you I called on Max Morrison."

"But the police don't know that."

"They do now. Lynch will point out the connection. They will ask what I was doing in Hertfordshire. I will have to admit I called on him. It wasn't a crime."

"What happened?"

"I can't tell you. You have promised to talk to Lynch."

"I promised nothing of the kind. I only said I'd tell him if you called. I haven't, have I?"

"Not yet, certainly."

"I shan't. Not so long as you are here. Do you believe me?"

Mr Robinson got up and stood in front of her, looking at her intently. She felt a stirring inside her and had a sense of helpless confusion. Mr Lynch and Max Morrison were irrelevant. Why had she drunk so much?

Mr Robinson, however, said only, "I do. I believe you," and returned to his seat.

Miss Kelly started to poke at the fire; it had been blazing and her efforts—she was trembling—succeeded only in smothering the flame. When she at last put down the poker, she turned to Mr Robinson—still on her knees—and said, "Will you tell me about Max now? I don't care if you frightened him. It was time somebody did; and you didn't know about his heart; how could you have?"

Mr Robinson said nothing, and Miss Kelly could only put on more fuel to repair the destruction she had done in the grate. Then she sat down again. Only an hour ago, she had felt elegant and poised, mistress in her own house; and now she was all flushes and confusion. Mr Robinson was examining his nails, but he had evidently been waiting for Miss Kelly to leave the fire alone, because he began at once.

"If you read the file, Miss Kelly, you must know that I changed my name. Max used to tease me about it. He liked to air his superior knowledge and culture. And whenever introductions were taking place he loved to say:

"My name is Norval; on the Grampian Hills
My father tends his flocks . . ."

He was showing off; the quotation is from an old play called
Douglas, no one except himself had ever heard of. It was extraordinary how he could make such a silly thing a way of wound-
ing. He did me infinite harm, that man; my mother was mad,
but Max was corrupt and evil and unscrupulous, no heart at all;
he would rob a canary's cage, nothing was beneath his notice
where his own advantage was concerned. He wanted my mother
dead, and when I told him she was dead, he washed his hands of
me, and left me to face it alone; and yet, when I used to think
about him afterwards, it was not that, nor his putting me out in
the street, nor his obscenity in my mother's house that used to
make me long to walk on his face, it was the times he used to say
'My name is Norval'—the *contempt* in his voice.

"And I will tell you now what happened in Hertfordshire. I
found out that he was living in Ashwell, a pretty village, in the
house he had acquired with his wife. I hired a car in London and
went down to spy out the land. I found a hotel in Old Stevenage,
a few miles away; I did not want to leave any traces of my visit in
Ashwell. Max was always a creature of settled habits, and I
knew, once I located his house, that I had only to watch it for a
day to acquaint myself with his routine.

"There was a pub almost opposite his door, and I made use of
this for spying purposes when it was open. There was no sign of
life in the house—I arrived at eight o'clock—and I parked my car
so as to keep his front gate in view. I sat there until twelve
o'clock and then he emerged, by himself, leading some sort of
little fancy dog. He had changed very little. When I knew him it
was difficult to make out whether he was a terribly old-looking
youth or a monstrously youthful old man. Now his face fitted.
He looked like a marmoset. Very watchful, sharp little eyes,
mouth drooping at the corners. As he passed—I was on the far
side of the road—he shot a glance in my direction, and I decided
not to be there when he came back. By that time I was sitting in
the window of the pub, and I had plenty of time to study him
while he waited on his dog who was piddling against a tree

159

trunk. This happened every day, I felt sure. And when he went in, he would cook himself an omelette and serve it up very prettily.

"I walked and drove about and sat in the car and in the pub, when it opened again, but Max never reappeared.

"I decided then to leave the village, in case anyone had seen me during the day, and return after night-fall. I drove to Hitchin, had dinner in a hotel there, and drove back to Ashwell.

"There was no light to be seen in Max's windows, but I had no doubt he was at home. I knocked and rang loudly, as he always used to do. I hoped it put the fear of God into him, but then he might have been afraid to open the door. What was I going to do if he asked who was there before he let me in? I hadn't provided for that. However, someone was at the door. It half opened. I could see a hall most elegantly furnished behind Max's head. He was poised to slam the door in my face, when he said, 'Who is it?' staring up at me, not knowing me from Adam. He sounded petulant, but I believe he was more hopeful that somebody had come to keep him company than fearful of a burglar. Now at last, I had the opportunity for which I had waited for forty years."

"Don't. Don't tell me." Miss Kelly had turned away, hiding her face. Mr Robinson took her head between his hands and stared into her frightened eyes.

"I looked at him as I am looking at you now, I answered his question. 'My name is Norval; on the Grampian Hills My father tends his flocks.'

"A knife into his throat or a shot between the eyes, couldn't have been a quicker weapon. His eyes opened very wide; his mouth opened very wide; he staggered back, and when I came into the hall, he was on the ground. I didn't touch him. I stood perfectly still. He made a few faint sounds, but not for very long. I waited for an hour exactly (there was a grandfather clock in the hall. Its tick was the only sound in the house). Then I went out. I think that was the happiest hour in my life."

Miss Kelly's lips were moving, but no sound came out of them. "Thank God, thank God," she was saying to herself; but Mr Robinson was unaware; his eyes were not seeing her or, perhaps, in her eyes he saw reflected a short broad hallway, an oriental rug on the parquet flooring, and on the rug the hunched figure of his friend. He let go Miss Kelly's head which, at the crisis of his account, he had pressed between his hands as if it were a concertina; now he was punching the palm of one hand with the fist of the other. Of Miss Kelly he remained unaware until he had given up the celebration of his lethal *riposte*, then he turned and discovered her beside him on the sofa.

"You must forgive me," he said, "but it was worth waiting forty years for that moment."

"Oh, you have no idea how relieved I am. For one awful moment I thought you were going to tell me you hit him or something. You are so strong and he sounds as if he were made of *papier mâché*. Why don't you tell Mr Lynch the story, just as you told it to me; but don't let him see you took such pleasure in it. I understand because I know what a villain the man was, but other people mightn't. It would look as if you had no feelings. I know you have, very strong ones; but it is always as well not to give the wrong impression."

"Lynch wouldn't believe me."

"Why not?"

"Because of something I once told him."

"What was that, may I ask? Don't glare at me, please, Mr Robinson. You have no idea how fierce you look."

"He told you?"

"I don't know what you are talking about."

"Did he say I admitted my guilt to him?"

"If you did, you were so bewildered and forsaken at the time, so much under the influence of Max Morrison and the Dostoevsky play, you literally didn't know the difference between what you imagined and reality."

"Did you tell him that?"

"We didn't discuss the matter. I read the report of the trial. Mr Lynch is an admirable person in many ways, but he never had the education it requires to understand such a complicated state of mind as yours was. Quite frankly, there was a time when I shouldn't have understood it either. I'd have said that it was all too high falutin' an excuse. Michael would not have listened to

161

it for a moment, and he was very nearly head boy at school, at Downside.

"I've learnt a lot since I met you, Mr Robinson. I've come to see how narrow and intolerant my attitudes were; as you said very cruelly but truly, mine has been a doll's house existence. I seem to have grown up in the last few weeks. I didn't read the whole account of the trial, by the way, only your evidence—"

"I didn't give evidence. I wasn't called."

"But I read—"

"That was the statement I madly gave to Lynch. If I had kept my mouth shut, there was no proof my mother died, and as her body was never discovered, I couldn't have been found guilty of her murder. Lynch had an extraordinary effect on me. I had found myself in Raskolnikov, and Lynch became the examining magistrate as soon as I talked to him, equally friendly and intelligent. In that character I was destined or (if you prefer) doomed to confess to him. But in my own wretched obscurity as Nevil Norval, he was the friend I needed, the substitute for my inadequate father. You see, I really longed to tell my father *everything*; he was the only person who understood the situation at home and about my mother; we really saw eye to eye about her; and when he was giving evidence I thought he was trying his best to help me. She had tried to ruin his life; he was glad to think she was dead and could bother him no longer. Even if he believed I had killed her, he knew that between us both we had suffered enough to justify it. Did I ever tell you why he left her?"

"No. You said she was foolishly jealous."

"Quite so. She was always making scenes and accusing his secretaries of having designs on him. She even rang up women clients to enquire if he was with them. There was a certain woman who was rather demanding. He had to be very much at her beck and call. My mother decided they were having an affair, and what did she do but put senna pods in his coffee at lunch when he said he was calling on her that afternoon. I heard her tell her friends about it on the telephone. 'That will put the kibosh on his little romance,' she said."

"Senna pods, why? Oh, I see." Miss Kelly flushed.

"He found the bottle in the kitchen, and when he accused her of dosing him, she admitted it, and laughed. He left her after that. He didn't see the funny side of it. I don't think she would have killed him, though.

"He couldn't face me after her death. He wouldn't have known what to say. And then, of course, the publicity of the trial and my disgrace were a lot to bear for a man who had already been through so much. He left the country almost at once. I wish I could have seen him before he died. If only I could have convinced him as I've managed to convince you, Miss Kelly."

"Oh, you *have* convinced me. But I never believed you committed the murder. Never. I saw what the false accusation had done to you. Tell me one thing: you said you were looking for the characters in *Crime and Punishment*. There was this girl who tried to rescue you. She wanted to go into exile with you. Didn't she? She was Sonia in the book, wasn't she? By then you had all the principal characters, and you had re-enacted the play. Did this Sonia redeem you? Tell me. I can't help being curious about her. What happened to her? Where is she now?"

"I haven't the least idea is the answer to the last question. You are very curious about her, aren't you? What does she matter? The attempt to rescue me failed, and it would have made me a fugitive for the rest of my life if it had succeeded. As it was, the doctors decided I had recovered after a few years and I was let go free. As sane as the day I went in, not less nor more. Is anyone perfectly sane, Miss Kelly? Are you?"

"I should hope so."

"But has your sanity ever been put to the test? You have been preserved in aspic all your life. Your money, your gentility, your religion, your education and your conservative tempera-ment—your law-abiding temperament, I should say—these have kept you out of harm's way. If you ever wanted anything very badly and couldn't get it—could you become irrational then? Don't answer that question. You don't know. Take that girl you mentioned just now. She wasn't Sonia. Sonia for me was the actress who was taking the part, who complained to Maurice Elvery because she objected to my staring at her during

163

rehearsals. I asked her to tea once. I never told you that. I never told anyone. She came. Max was out. I chose a Sunday when I knew he would be at one of his grand parties. I couldn't believe it when she said yes. Maurice Elvery's leading lady! It seemed beyond the wildest possibility that she would condescend to have afternoon tea with me. I imagined her entertaining a bevy of contending suitors, like Portia. Not granting her favours to any of them. They were too precious for that. A talented young Dublin actress at the very beginning of her career—to me she was a great star. I had bought supplies and hidden them with great difficulty. I didn't want Max to know. I was afraid of his mockery. I didn't want him to soil a sacred occasion—it was, for me—with tittering questions; and he would certainly have quizzed her about it and pretended that I had told him all about her visit. He was also quite capable of picking a quarrel with me about my extravagance. I had spent about five shillings on the preparations.

"I would never have had the courage to invite her—it would have required courage even if she had not already complained about me—but I was bowled over when she talked to me nicely when by chance we were left alone between rehearsals. She had a very engaging manner, and seemed to be interested in the flat, when I told her about it. I invited her to come and see for herself. And she accepted. It didn't occur to me that she was merely curious, and I might have known that she had been there in the past. I thought she was sympathetic, and in a way I believe she was. Everyone had Max's number, and I was probably seen as a victim.

"When she came I was delighted by her interest. I showed her everything. She was standing at the bedroom door. 'May I take a peep?' she said. I said 'Of course', and let her go in by herself.

" 'Very nice,' she said, coming out.

"If I told Max about this I could imagine what he would have said, and I suddenly felt embarrassed about the bedroom. Of course, it was all part of her curiosity about Max's arrangements, and had nothing to do with her and me. Not that for a moment would I have contemplated such a thing. I was overcome with respect for her, and I had no experience with women.

164

"She rather nannied me in her talk, and she helped to make the tea. But as soon as it was finished, she looked at her watch and gave an exclamation. How time had flown, she said. How much she had enjoyed herself. She was in and out in an hour and a half. When she had gone I ate every crumb of cake that was left over and a packet of sweet biscuits. I wasn't going to leave any evidence for Max to gloat over.

"I was in ecstasy. I had found my Sonia. She was mine in reality, as I had willed it and dreamed it. I made plans in my mind for meeting her behind Max's back. Would she invite me to her place? Now that I knew her destiny I had no fear of rivals.

"Quite sanguine, I went up to her at once next day in the theatre; she was in a group and made no reference to her visit; when I tried to single her out she said, 'Can't you see I'm talking to someone?' She sounded cross. I couldn't understand the transformation. Not that her manner had changed from what it had usually been towards me; some days she had smiled, on others she had been preoccupied. But that had ended for ever yesterday, I thought. I had mistaken her passing whim for an acceptance of her rôle in my fantasy. Now it seems incredible. It didn't at the time. Then came the *dénouement*; my arrest, Max's refusal to help, Lynch in the rôle of the examining magistrate, the trial. After that, this other girl appeared. She came to the trial, never missed a day, wrote me letters of devotion and sympathy, sent me presents, fainted when the jury brought in the verdict.

"She organised the attempt to rescue me. I was glad to hear that she found helpers in the theatre. They believed me guilty, but said my mother deserved it.

"There is all the difference in the world between the word and the deed, Miss Kelly. When I think of what I lived in imagination and compare it with the reality of my mother's corpse I want to destroy all the books, plays, films, television sets that feed the world with their fantasies."

Mr Robinson rose to his feet and as he embraced the crowded shelves with his baleful glance, Miss Kelly had a pang of fear for her property. But the moment passed. He sat down, but not beside her this time, and seemed to be brooding. Miss Kelly deemed it wise to be silent and tried to retrace her mental steps to where she had enquired about this girl who had been so much in love with Mr Robinson. Did she start off with him when he went into exile? And if so, what had happened? Ever since the time Mr Robinson forgot who she was and behaved so strangely in the motor car, she was morbidly curious to know whom she had reminded him of and what precisely had happened to *her* on a similar occasion. If it was anything she shouldn't know about, she didn't want to know, she told herself; she merely desired to know whom she had impersonated. It was hurtful to vanity to be told she belonged to a class of women distinguished only by having in common a resemblance to Mr Robinson's mother. That, in her case, had certainly aroused Mr Robinson's interest in her; but she had subsequently impressed her own personality on him. He had said so. He called her his only friend.

She couldn't get away from the subject.

"What did this girl who tried to rescue you look like?"

"She was dark and tall and pale and skinny, not in the least like you."

"And not like Sonia—not like the actress who played Sonia, I mean."

"Even less like her. It was Peggy Leitch, you may remember her; she was *petite* and baby-faced."

"I do remember her. I saw her act with Maurice Elvery on several occasions. She was attractive. I can well understand her fascination for you."

"I saw her as Sonia, not as a girl who attracted me. In her rôle I loved her; but in life I was not attracted by women. I will tell you something Miss Kelly, you will hardly believe. When I first saw my mother's dead body what do you think I thought of? Meat. Women are only meat. After that it was easy to do whatever I had to. I suppose a butcher's apprentice and a young medical student in the dissecting room feel very much the same about the material they work on."

He was trying to shock her, Miss Kelly knew. He was trying to kill in her the sympathy he had seemed to need and crave. But she wouldn't allow this to happen now when he had failed with

166

his rudeness and roughness. She must get through to the wounded heart underneath the carapace. He had not been able to hide his emotional hunger. She had seen it in his eyes.

"Don't talk like that, please."

"You are responsible for it, pestering me about that girl."

"I'm sorry if I pestered you. I only—"

"Women always want to know about their predecessors. Let me tell you that creature had only one useful purpose. She cured me of my dreaming habit. She was no Sonia; she had no desire to redeem me. She loved me for what she thought I had done. She was filled with desire for a youth who could murder his mother. I was her Playboy, and she preferred hers to the one in the play because the other had axed only his father, and I had removed at one stroke a parent and a rival. She had her hero all to herself if she could get him out of the clutches of the law. Believe me, she was as anxious that my story be true as you were to hear it was not. What would you say if I went back on my story, if I told you I had been telling you lies, that I did kill my mother, took the axe from the wood-shed and felled her as if she were a cow? What would you say if I told you that? Come on. Don't look as if you had seen a ghost. Tell me what you are thinking."

"I think you are very cruel. I can't understand you. Why do you behave like this to me. I've tried to help you. You said I had done more for you than anyone."

"Because I believe you did it for the same reason that all women do these things. You want me to become dependent on you. You want to eat me alive. Yes, you do. Underneath all that refinement of yours, Miss Kelly, is the woman's usual equipment, nature's weapons. Be honest. Strip that nice dress off. Look at yourself. And if I were not proof against those weapons, what would have happened to me? That crazy girl heard I had been released. She followed me across the world—What's that? There's someone at the door. I heard the bell."

He came beside Miss Kelly and held her arms. "Don't answer it."

The bell continued to ring. Then, after a pause, whoever it was knocked very loudly. Miss Kelly looked imploringly at her jailer, but he only tightened his grip.

167

Then came sounds in the house and soon after of a chain being taken off the front door and voices.

"Take your hands away. Mrs Ridley will be coming in."

She came in at that instant.

"It's the Sergeant from Swords. He would like a word with you."

"I'll come out to him," Miss Kelly said, getting up. She didn't look at Mr Robinson. Mrs Ridley stood aside to let her pass and then closed the door. The Sergeant was standing in the hall.

"Good evening, Sergeant, what can I do for you?"

"I'm sorry for calling at this hour of the night, but I happened to be passing, and I thought I might drop in to ask you if you have heard anything from Mr Robinson, who has been staying in Malahide recently. I believe he is back in this country. If you see him would you please ask him to be good enough to give me a call. He hasn't been in touch with you, by any chance? I hate to be bothering you like this, but he might be able to help us in a little trouble we are having, if we could get in touch with him."

"I thought Mr Robinson—if it's the same person—was in England. He was here quite recently, and he said nothing about coming back."

"Well, if he does, give him my message, and, if it's not too much trouble, would you ring me up? You will always find me at the barracks. He might forget, and I do need his help."

Miss Kelly, in the ordinary course, would not have left this caller standing in the hall, and she thought his eyes looked thoughtful as they left hers to rest on the door of the library and then returned to meet hers again with nothing said by either of them.

"I was just going to bed."

"It's lucky I caught you. I won't hold you up any longer, and I apologise again for disturbing you at this hour of the night."

It was, in fact, only a few minutes to ten.

"Goodbye, Sergeant."

"Goodnight, Ma'am, and thank you kindly."

Miss Kelly stood at the door and raised a hand slightly in token of farewell.

She paused at the library door before opening it to gather resolution; she had been astonished by herself, the facility with which she had all but lied to the Sergeant was bad enough, but the possibility that he suspected as much was worse. Since her birth, she had been taught that only the lower orders were untruthful; it was the Irish disease. Like the discovery that grown-ups put their elbows on the table, she learned in time that lying was not confined to a class any more than failure to keep promises—it was a character, not a class, distinction—but to be put in this humiliating position with the local Sergeant, a man she allowed to stand in her hall, was intolerable. Had Mr Robinson not been inside, she would undoubtedly have invited the Sergeant to come into the library (a mere Guard would have been spoken to in the hall). The Sergeant might have sensed that she had company—hence the place of interview—and was reasonably curious in the circumstances to know of what it consisted. Lucky that Mr Robinson had the foresight to park his car in the yard! And, no doubt, the Sergeant would now ring Mr Lynch, and the roads would be watched. It would not be safe for Mr Robinson to leave for the present. But why did she have to say she was on her way to bed? It would have been more convincing to explain that she was entertaining friends. In the circumstances the Sergeant would not have expected to be invited in. She could have told the truth, and it would have been more effective than the lie, which he may have sensed. It hung in the air for Miss Kelly, like Macbeth's dagger. She didn't tell lies, and her bluntness was attributed to stupidity, which was unfair. Lack of imagination, however, made it easier not to substitute fiction for fact.

She had made her greatest sacrifice to date for Mr Robinson. She had lost her integrity. She was in league with him against the law. And she was not going to allow him to bully her.

Resolved, she went into the library and confronted a glance of disapproval.

"Where have you been?"

"You know very well."

"I heard the car drive away a few minutes ago."

"If you did, I haven't to account to you for every second of my time. Who do you think you are?"

He flushed. She held her pose. He swallowed his sudden anger. It was Miss Kelly's first winning round in their long contest. She decided to follow it up.

"If you want to know, the Sergeant said he was looking for you. He said if I saw you I was to tell you to ring up the barracks. I could see from his manner that he suspected someone was with me, and I'd like to think, for my own sake, that he didn't guess it was you. I'm glad you thought of hiding your car."

"If he thought you had visitors, it must have seemed odd there was no car outside; and how do we know what your servant told him?"

"How can I ask her?"

"And will she tell the truth?"

"Mrs Ridley is a most superior woman. I'd never question what she told me."

"No doubt, the Sergeant has the same opinion of her mistress."

"I might be able to help if you would tell me what you want to do. You can't live here or in England if you are trying to avoid the police. Would you be safe in Australia? Should you go home and let this fuss die down? Why did you come back this time?"

"To see you."

"You don't expect me to believe that."

"I can't get you out of my mind. You haunt me."

"But you don't trust me."

"I do, as much as I can trust anyone. The first person I ever wholly trusted was Lynch. For that, I was sent to a lunatic asylum. I don't blame him. He was doing his duty. But I had never felt so close to anyone as I did to him. He was what my father should have been, what my friend should have been. He understood what I said. He wasn't shocked. He treated me like a human being, an equal. He was everything that I would like to have been—confident, easy, authoritative. I saw how his men respected him. I wanted him to accept me, and I tried to impress him, tried so hard that I handed myself over to the law. I was so confused I did not see, even if I made him my friend, that he had his job to do. Now he is your friend; he is concerned for your safety; he has brought himself out of retirement to protect you. And from me. That is the irony of it. He must believe you are threatened. Now, tell me, what has given him that impression? What did you say about me to him? You must have said something or you wouldn't have had the Sergeant here this evening."

"You know what happened. You told me to get the file for you. I am not going back over that again. The coincidence of Max Morrison's death and your visit to him, that's what made him suspicious. Your calling first on me, then on Max."

"So you told him I called on Max."

"How could I have? I didn't know where you were. You left no address. I had to tell Mr Lynch how I had met you because I couldn't otherwise explain why I was acting on your behalf. If you had left him alone and forgotten about the file, this wouldn't have happened. It all springs from that. You told me to give him your letter to me and that was all about Max. I don't understand you. You do everything to put people's backs up and then say they are persecuting you. And you make a mystery of everything. Why not call on Mr Lynch and clear this matter up, even if it means seeing the police in England? Unless you do, you can't blame them for being suspicious. Ring Mr Lynch up now, say you are here. I'm sure he will believe your story, and then he will clear you with the English police."

"Very kind of him, having put them on my trail in the first place."

"Why did you rake all this terrible business up again? What good could you do? It was all over and forgotten, and now you are in trouble again, and I am in trouble too. And you don't trust me. It's my own fault. I should never have interfered. But I thought you needed help. I was desperately sorry for you. I—"

Mr Robinson smothered the last word. His arms were round Miss Kelly. Her face was buried in his shoulder. She wept her heart out. "God help me. God help me", were the only intelligible words that came out of the confused babbling against his chest. And they stayed thus, he neither moving nor speaking, until long after the fire died. Miss Kelly had fallen asleep by

171

then, and Mr Robinson extricated himself from underneath her substantial weight, putting a cushion under her head. Then he pulled back the curtains, and let the first light straggle in.

She woke up and seemed not to recognise him at first. Then she opened her mouth in astonishment, looked herself over as if she had been lying out-of-doors, then sat up suddenly.

"I must have fallen asleep," she said. "What time is it?" she added when he made no reply. Then she looked at her watch.

"My goodness, it's five o'clock." And as he still said nothing, she turned to the fire and coaxed it into flame. This gave her an opportunity to collect her resources. She had a confused recollection of breaking down and of Mr Robinson's putting his arms round her, of being at last where she wanted to be, of telling him secrets which seemed to come from somewhere inside her that she was unaware of.

When she looked up, she was smiling. "You must have made up your mind by now. What are you going to do?"

"At eight o'clock, you are going to ring Lynch up, tell him about the Sergeant's call, say I was here, say you were afraid to say so in case I should hear you. And you can say I left soon afterwards. Lynch will ask why you didn't ring up at once. Tell him there was no reason to wake him up to say you were safe and well. It was time enough at breakfast. You can say that you are quite satisfied Max Morrison died from the effect his bad conscience had on his bad heart. And that is literally the truth."

"But the rest is lies."

"I was going. You prevented me."

"And what will you do?"

"I'll lie low for the present. When you are talking to Lynch, ask him to explain your conduct to the Sergeant. Say you are too embarrassed to do that yourself."

"And what if he calls?"

"Who?"

"Either of them."

"You can repeat the story."

"And what am I to tell them about your visit?"

"Just what I told you. Stick to the truth. I'm sorry I have to ask you to improve on it in one particular."

172

"Well, you had better go to your room. Mrs Ridley is always stirring by half-past seven. I told her to bring you a cup of early morning tea at eight. Breakfast is at half-past, unless you would like it in bed."

"I'll stay in bed. And please cancel that early morning tea. I hope I'll be asleep by then."

This was all so unexpected and pleasant, Miss Kelly became mildly euphoric. Eccentric though he remained, Mr Robinson had all the instincts of a gentleman. If only she could persuade him to be courageous about this Max Morrison business, there would be nothing to interfere with their friendship. And if not, if he ran away and invited her to come with him, would she? Would she? The question could only be answered when the moment came. She had learnt that much about herself.

As soon as Mr Robinson had gone to his room, she undressed and went to bed, setting an alarm clock for a quarter-past seven; but she couldn't sleep and long before that she ran herself a bath. She lay in it, her mind turned off, vaguely happy, expectant. She took time selecting the clothes she would wear. From lack of anything to occupy her mind clothes played a large part in her life. She always had far more than she could wear, and many dresses worn once, or not at all, hung in her wardrobes.

Nothing seemed right today. And her face when she looked at herself in the glass was none the better for the adventures of the night. She made it up with exemplary care, and then, encouraged by the result, put on a boyish shirt and a trouser suit. She had a good figure, a good figure for her age. All this took time, but when Mrs Ridley appeared with tea, she was able to tell her not to wake Mr Robinson. It was close on nine o'clock when she came downstairs; she felt better able to deal with Mr Lynch now. She was her old self again and something more. She was actually humming when she came into the dining-room.

Mr Robinson was sitting at the table in front of a plate of rashers and eggs. He got up when Miss Kelly came in, wiping his mouth with a napkin.

"I rang Lynch up," he said. "I decided that was the best course. I told him we would call tomorrow morning at his place, and if the Sergeant would like to make a meal of it, he could come as well. If you come with me, I think we should be a match for them."

Miss Kelly listened: her face turned pink; she went up to Mr Robinson and kissed him full on the lips.

"Oh, I am *so* glad. Now we can stop worrying. After all, you have nothing to fear. Mr Lynch raised the matter on my account. Now he *must* be satisfied."

Mr Robinson never rose to Miss Kelly's occasions, and she was disappointed, but not surprised, to see a look of doubt pass over his pale face.

"They may try to say I'm mad. Lynch could still want to keep me away from you."

"He hasn't the authority to do that. I can get the best doctors in Dublin—in London, for that matter, if anyone tries tricks of that sort. But I believe this is only your imagination. And no wonder, considering what was done to you."

"Lynch will want to justify that. He must have qualms. For the comfort of his conscience it is necessary that he should believe I was mad at the time, and if he can prove I am mad now, it strengthens his case. That is why he has allowed himself to get so worked up about you. There is nobody so dangerous as a really good man when he has to justify himself to his own conscience. Lynch doesn't want to go to his grave with my wrongful conviction on his soul; it would be more comfortable to feel that he has come out of retirement as a knight in armour to protect a fair lady. St George and the Dragon."

"I think you are making it all sound more complicated than it is," Miss Kelly said. Flights of fancy never appealed to her. "You would have been better advised not to trouble Mr Lynch about that file in the first instance. All our troubles began when I called on him. That was your plan, but I am not going to allow anything to spoil the day. What time did you say our appointment is tomorrow?"

"Eleven o'clock."

"Good. Afterwards, you and I will go somewhere nice for lunch. There's a hotel in Delgany, quite close to the house."

The morning went slowly. Mr Robinson was shown round the garden. He had very little to say. When they met Donnelly,

174

who was cutting raspberry canes, Miss Kelly remembered the last occasion when the three of them were together. She had a short conversation with her workman while Mr Robinson stood by. He never indulged in random civilities, and on this occasion, if he had passed the time of day, it might have relieved Miss Kelly's embarrassment. Donnelly's tact saved the situation. He behaved as if there were only two people present and Mr Robinson were a tree.

"Mr Duggan called at my place this morning, ma'am. He's lost a ewe, and he said Lupin was responsible for it. It's a great pity he caught him that time last year. He's had it in for the creature ever since."

"I hope you said Lupin was kept locked up at night."

"I did; but when a man the like of Duggan gets an idea into his head, it's hard to shift him. He said he'd be getting in touch with you; so I'm telling you in time. He has the ewe lying out in the fields for the Guards to see. I told him he had a right to bring it into the stables. But there's no use in talking to him."

"Lupin, did you kill Mr Duggan's ewe?" Miss Kelly addressed the dog, who looked innocent of crime.

"Where did this happen? Is it anywhere near the shore?" Mr Robinson sounded excited.

"Beside it, sir. Where you had the car the first time I seed you," Donnelly replied.

This discouraged Mr Robinson, and he seemed preoccupied when Miss Kelly wanted to discuss the extent of the threat to her retriever. It would have helped to pass the time if they could have gone out, but by tacit consent no move from the house and grounds was contemplated until it was time for the encounter with the enemy.

Once, in the garden, Miss Kelly took Mr Robinson's hand; but it lay in hers like an empty glove. He gave the impression of not liking to be touched. Miss Kelly understood, Michael had been like that. She was rather like that herself as a rule; but ever since last night she wanted to touch Mr Robinson all the time, and she was waiting for the moment when he would put his arms round her as he had in the library. That had knocked down the

175

last barricade so far as she was concerned. If he attacked, she was defenceless now.

"I think I shall lie down for a little," Mr Robinson said after lunch.

"I think that would be a very good thing. You didn't get a wink of sleep last night. I'll put a hot-water bottle in your bed, and I shouldn't move if I were you until dinner time. You will need to be on the very top of your form for tomorrow."

Nothing could have been so natural and encouraging as Miss Kelly's manner. She didn't listen when Mr Robinson muttered some deprecatory remark about hot-water bottles. She filled one herself, and turned down the bed, and put the bottle in, selecting the strategic spot.

"There," she said, and turned round briskly, hoping to find him beside her; but he was checking the contents of his wallet absorbedly, and paying no attention to the preparations for his comfort.

"Sleep well. No one will disturb you," Miss Kelly said at the door.

"I'll see you later," Mr Robinson replied, and smiled, but not with his eyes.

Nothing could dampen Miss Kelly's spirits. Downstairs she designed a dinner which required a call on the butcher, and she did not hesitate to drive to the village to choose the cut she had in mind. There followed a delicious consultation with Mrs Ridley, who would have to do all the boring parts of the business. Miss Kelly prepared a delicious first course, for which she had never divulged the recipe. What would they drink? Nothing obviously celebratory. A very good claret; that might be best. She went to the cellar herself. Michael's laying down was beginning to look rather thin. In a way, this was symbolic. A new era was dawning. It would provide its own wine.

She picked late roses, stripping the trees, and put them in vases everywhere. In comparison with the morning's slow progress, the afternoon raced by.

At seven o'clock, she went to Mr Robinson's door—she was bathed and dressed by then—and waited and listened and then knocked. Once gently, then a little louder. No reply. She waited and knocked quite hard. Her knuckles hurt.

"Mr Robinson," she called. She knocked again. Then she opened the door very gently. The room was empty.

The bed had been slept in. His things were in the room. He had not taken flight. The hot-water bottle lay on the floor.

The prosaic possibility that he was in the lavatory occurred to her, but his dressing-gown was lying across a chair. No sound came from the bathroom.

She ran downstairs, breathless, and looked in each room. Then she went out and round the house to the yard. His car stood in the coach house. She gave a gasp of relief. Attempting a casual tone, she asked Mrs Ridley, in the kitchen, busy, if she happened to have seen Mr Robinson. Mrs Ridley had not. Miss Kelly went out again. He was definitely not in the grounds.

She rushed into the house, looked again into his room, called his name, and was about to panic when she looked out of an upper window and saw him walking slowly along the road towards the gate lodge. Had he looked up he would have seen her gazing down as that other time at the guest house in Donegal, but he was evidently too much interested in his own thoughts. He went past the front door and then pushed open the french windows of the drawing-room. This simple action filled Miss Kelly with awe. She sat on her bed and pondered long; deciding finally not to pretend she knew he had been out of doors until he mentioned it. With anyone else it would be the most commonplace matter to take a stroll before dinner, certainly not worth mentioning; but Mr Robinson's habitual secretiveness lent to his every action something of mystery. She looked again at her face, touched it here and there, put scent behind her ears, and went downstairs.

In the drawing-room, Mr Robinson was examining the pictures. He looked up and then resumed his inspection.

"That is supposed to be a rather good Hone," Miss Kelly said. "My father made quite a collection of his pictures. I like the one in the hall best; but then I never care for seascapes." Her fingers were on Mr Robinson's arm, but so as he might have hardly noticed, as if by accident. He said nothing and continued

177

to stare at the picture. He never showed pleasure when he looked at things. He turned away, still keeping his counsel. Miss Kelly beamed at him.

"What would you like to drink? Help yourself. And I am going to take a very little whiskey; but you must promise not to tell anyone."

"Whom could I tell?"

"I was only joking. Whiskey before dinner seems rather depraved to me. I know Americans drink it; but they don't know anything about wine."

"I dare say some of them do," Mr Robinson said.

"That's much too much," she protested when he came back with a tumbler half-full. "A third of that, and then fill it up with water."

"Go on," he said. "It will do you no harm."

"No. Please. It would only spoil my dinner."

He did as he was told, and then helped himself.

"How are you feeling after your rest? You needed it," she ventured.

"Quite well. Thank you."

He looked round the room as if hoping to find a topic lying about. He had no small talk, Miss Kelly decided, and that would make social life difficult. It took getting used to; she saw that, and it would be easier when Mr Robinson relaxed and seemed to be more at home. But what she was waiting for was a reference to his solitary walk. It was unfriendly of him not to mention it. Was he regretting his last night's behaviour? Was he afraid that he had compromised himself? She wished now that she was more experienced with men. Except to show that she was happy, she could think of no other way to put him at ease. But she must watch herself; he was so unpredictable. That girl who pursued him may have put him off women. Miss Kelly wanted to hear more about that. Above all, she was curious about that other woman, who had been much closer to him. What had happened to her?

Mrs Ridley came in and said dinner was ready. Miss Kelly took Mr Robinson's arm playfully and led him into the dining-room. The table certainly looked brilliant; the best of the Kelly glass and silver was on display and the Worcester dinner service. Most effective of all, the centre bowl in which rose heads were floating.

Miss Kelly's eyes sparkled. Her grip tightened for a brief moment on Mr Robinson's sleeve. The effect called for a cheer. He kept his counsel. At dinner she drank too fast and lit cigarettes between courses, took a few pulls on each and lit another. Whenever she heard her own voice she became mildly desperate. She was alarmed at her recklessness when, without any action of her own will, she heard herself saying:

"Where did you walk to this afternoon?"

"Only so far as the estuary."

"Did you see any swans?"

"I don't think so, why?"

"It's full of them."

"Yes. That's true. I remember."

"I hope you had a good sleep."

"I had. Thank you."

"What time did you go out?"

"I really can't remember."

"I asked only because I didn't hear you."

And when he made no reply to that, she said, "I can't tell you how happy I was all day. I know you made the right decision this morning. We shan't know ourselves by this time tomorrow. I know what I would like to do then."

"What would you like to do then?"

"Buy us tickets straight away for a cruise. I don't know where would be best to go at this time of year. I want us both to forget all this trouble. I have a little money on deposit that I don't know what to do with. I can't think of any better way of spending it. What do you say?"

"I think we should first make sure that I will be free to travel."

"Of course, you will. What can I do for you to get you to look at the brighter side. Have some more to drink. There's very little left in that bottle. You might as well finish it up."

She filled Mr Robinson's glass and stood beside his chair. Looking down on his head, she felt an impulse to caress it.

"You mustn't worry, dear man," she said quickly. "Let me be your friend. No one will hurt you this time." She did not linger. He had just enough time to put his arm round her waist and give a responding squeeze, had he wished to. But he hadn't. She picked a too large handful of grapes out of the fruit bowl and ate them like a child.

Mr Robinson looked steadily into his glass, and then, as if he had calculated the effort required, emptied it in one draught.

"Let's go into the library. The coffee's there," she said.

Not waiting for his agreement, she got up, and moved towards the door, smiling. The first act had not fulfilled her expectations, but she was suspending judgement until the second was over. At least the dinner had been a good one; and he had eaten it all. Michael would have had a stroke if he had seen that claret being swallowed like beer by navvies on a building site; but, even so, only the best was good enough for tonight.

The firelight in the library was comforting; they hardly needed any other, she decided. She settled herself on the hearthrug from where she could dispense the coffee from the tray on the sofa table.

Mr Robinson chose the armchair which put the width of the hearth between them. Had he preferred it, he could have taken the other end and had her head against his knee. She poured out his brandy for him. Then, to give the final touch of slippered ease, she threw a log on the already cheerful fire.

Mrs Ridley had been trained not to knock on doors, but she must have decided that the circumstances of this evening were exceptional. She tapped once, waited, and then came in. She looked agitated.

"Donnelly's in the kitchen, Miss Kelly, he wants a word with you."

"At this time of night?"

"He says it's to do with Lupin and Mr Duggan's sheep."

"But can't that wait very well till tomorrow?"

"He says the Guards were with him."

"Damn," Miss Kelly said. "Ask him to come in then."

Mrs Ridley looked at Mr Robinson and then at Miss Kelly.

"Very well, Miss."

"I'm sorry about this," Miss Kelly said when Mrs Ridley went out. "Help yourself to brandy. It might be better if I talked to Donnelly in the kitchen."

She got up quickly, lurched slightly, and ignored Mr Robinson's call for her to stay. She felt unable to cope with Donnelly, the dog and Mr Robinson all at the same time.

Donnelly looked embarrassed enough when she found him in the kitchen, twisting a tweed cap in his huge hands.

"What is it now?" she asked, then turning to the dog who rushed up to her, "They are trying to take your character away, Lupin. I won't let them."

It was Michael who had insisted on dogs being kept outside. Miss Kelly felt a sudden urge to throw all rules to Hell. "They won't touch a hair of your head," she said to Lupin, kissing him.

"I'd like to speak to you private, ma'am," Donnelly said, at which Mrs Ridley walked out of the kitchen, closing the door behind her. Miss Kelly felt bellicose about the interruption of the evening, and the mention of Guards had done nothing to cheer her. Donnelly would take his time, having come to tell his story. She looked fretful.

"It's about the sheep."

"Did the Guards speak to you?"

"They did."

"Well, what did they say?"

"They were wondering if there was a gentleman staying in your place."

"What did you say?"

"I said I didn't know who was in the house. I worked in the grounds."

"And what about the sheep? What had they to say about that?"

"The sheep wasn't there when they came."

"That's very odd."

"I wonder was it on account of that they were asking about who was staying here."

"What has that got to do with it?"

"If they thought the gentleman took the sheep."

"I don't understand you."

181

"Someone might have said."

"That Mr Robinson took the sheep! How absurd!"

"The missus saw him."

"Mrs Donnelly saw Mr Robinson?"

"She did. She was in the long lane this afternoon and she saw the gentleman dragging the sheep along the jetty and letting it down into the water."

"Is she sure? I can't believe it. You didn't repeat Mrs Donnelly's story to the Guards?"

"No, ma'am. I didn't think it could do any good."

"Thank you very much. As you say, it couldn't have done any good."

"But you wouldn't know who else might have seen him. People are very nosy in these parts. And it's a queer thing for a grown man to do the like of that to a sheep."

"I'll have to look into it, I'm sure there's some explanation. You were very good to tell me. I'll be seeing Mrs Donnelly in a day or two. Now, I must go back; I have visitors. Thank you Donnelly. See that Lupin is shut in before you go, will you, in case anyone else should call."

She still found herself a little unsteady. She walked carefully. When she came back to the library, Mr Robinson was standing inside the door as if to waylay her.

"Take your hand away, please. I'm really very angry. What did you think you were doing today when you threw Mr Duggan's sheep into the sea? Do you realise how much embarrassment this will cause me? The Guards called on Donnelly this afternoon. He came to warn me. Apart from anything else, this man Duggan is convinced that Lupin chases his sheep. He caught him once in the field; and he's after his blood. But how am I to explain your behaviour?"

"Nobody saw me this afternoon."

"You are wrong there. Mrs Donnelly did. She told her husband."

"I was walking round the estuary when I came across this dead sheep lying on the side of the road. I didn't know how long it might have been there. I wanted to test the action of the tide, and I pulled it into the water. It was going to rot anyway."

182

"How can you go near that spot? I can't understand you. What are you trying to do?"

He didn't answer directly. Then he went and sat on the fender, staring into the fire, pulling his chin.

"Nobody saw my mother after she died except me. I saw her in the water, Miss Kelly. For five, ten minutes perhaps. What happened to her then? Where did she go? Was she dead? That's the question I ask myself."

Miss Kelly began to run her fingers through his hair. Frightened, as if she were stroking a wild animal, she could not hold back her hand. He took and held it.

"Come away," she whispered. "You must forget this. It is ruining your life. I'll stay with you. I'll help you. I have enough for us both."

"I don't want to get away. Everything is here. It's a sort of miracle. Consider, Miss Kelly, when I came back from Australia, I had only this vague plan of taking a last look at my Irish past. I thought of it as dead. My mother was dead, my father. I had no friends. The theatre people meant nothing to me. I had passed on from there. I had played a part none of them would have dared to play. Then, by chance, I went to Donegal and saw you, and you told me you had always lived beside the Swords estuary, and you were waiting for a visit from Cyril Forbes, friend of Max Morrison. I can't describe the effect it had on me. I couldn't believe it was mere coincidence. Once before I had an illusion that I had seen my mother. I must tell you this, because otherwise you won't understand my conduct. You must often think it inconsistent, but I have made such terrible mistakes in my life, the consequences have been so cruel; I am naturally suspicious of myself. This time it was quite different. I see you at the age my mother was when I——On the other occasion, when I made a mistake, I was astonished by the girl's likeness to photographs of my mother when she first grew up, before she knew my father. She was such a pretty girl. I have those photographs with me. I'd like to show them to you. They are in my room."

"Don't bother now. Another time, I'd love to see them."

"No trouble. None in the least. I've only to slip upstairs."

183

Mr Robinson didn't wait to argue. He was unusually animated; there was excitement in his eyes such as had not been present at dinner. It was not the way Miss Kelly had seen the evening develop. After last night and the day-long preparations, after that superb dinner and the priceless claret, to be looking at girlhood photographs of Mr Robinson's mother—his mother, with all that implied, whom she wished above all things this evening to forget—it was hard.

But she must humour him, and the fact remained, however gruesome, that the likeness to his mother was what had attracted Mr Robinson to her in the first place. Perhaps this was his way to approach her, a shy man's manoeuvre. He could say complimentary things about his mother's looks that he was too inhibited to say about her own.

It would be foolish not to fall in with his whim. They could not spend all evening looking at photographs. Pray God they were few. She looked up nervously when he came back with an envelope in his hand. He held it lovingly, and took out the contents with the eagerness of a collector. At least they were not many, Miss Kelly noticed with relief, and when Mr Robinson handed her the envelope she said, "Come here and show them to me," leading him to the sofa.

He dealt them out one by one, looking at each one before he passed it on. They had all been taken on the same occasion, a friend having come to tea armed with a camera. An afternoon of tea and tennis and croquet in a suburban garden before the First World War. Everyone looking incredibly dowdy.

"There she is. You can't see her face very clearly."

"That's a better one, it's a pity it has faded."

"She had lovely hair—you couldn't tell—under that hat."

"I like that best," Miss Kelly said, handing back one in which Mr Robinson's mother was smiling. "They are not very good pictures. I'm sure they don't do her justice."

"I wanted you to see them." Mr Robinson sounded slightly defensive.

"I was very glad to," she assured him. "Of course, I always think people in old photographs look as if they are wearing unbecoming fancy dress."

184

"Oh, do you think so!"

He sounded disappointed now, and took another look at some of them before putting them back into their envelope, which had that look peculiar to its kind of having been soaked in weak tea. Miss Kelly moved quickly to ward off the threat to the evening.

"Tell me about this girl, the one you made the mistake about. Did you fall in love with her?"

Mr Robinson crinkled his lips in distaste.

"I met her about twenty years ago. I had had a rather serious illness and my doctor advised me to go on a cruise to convalesce. There was this English girl on the ship; she had been visiting relatives in Australia, and was flirting with the ship's doctor. There was something about her which fascinated me, and it took me a few days to realise that it was a likeness to my mother in those photographs we have been looking at. I showed them to her. I don't think she saw the likeness, but we became better acquainted as a result of it."

"And what had the ship's doctor to say to that?"

"He resented it. That sort of chap expected to collect a scalp on every voyage. Part of his pickings. He was Irish, a university graduate on his first job, full of Dublin gossip. He must have seen my passport. I don't know how else he discovered what my name was. I always called myself Robinson. Kelly was his name; one of the hundreds of Kellys, but my wretched Norval was fatal. He told the girl all about me. He thought it would frighten her off. In fact it had the opposite effect. She wouldn't leave me alone. Can you believe it, Miss Kelly? I told her I was innocent. I told her the whole story, and I thought I had convinced her; but I learned subsequently that she didn't believe me. What sort of woman is that? Does she deserve to be called a woman? Now, do you understand what I felt when I saw you? I had first to reconcile myself to yet another woman's looking exactly like my mother, and after that, when we became friends, when I touched you, I remembered that other, and I felt I was never going to be allowed to escape from this degradation. For that is what it is."

"What degradation? What are you talking about? You are all

185

confused. You loved your mother in spite of everything. You have never recovered from her death. You have never been loved as you deserve. You must forget it all and those women who were part and parcel of it. Come away and see new places. Let me help you."

She put out a less timid hand now and touched Mr Robinson's chest. He was staring in front of him, and seemed oblivious to her presence.

"Don't stay locked up in the past. Look at me."

She took Mr Robinson's head in her hands and stared into his eyes. At first they seemed glazed, but suddenly his expression changed. He had solved whatever was perplexing him. He didn't try to extricate himself from Miss Kelly's hold, but looked at her from under his eyes in the manner that had startled her before—it was so calculating and detached. But it was for a moment.

"Tell me," he said quietly, "if you were to hear that I did it, would you still love me?"

"Did what?"

"You know. That I actually killed my mother."

"But you didn't. I've always known you didn't."

"I believe you; but suppose you discovered that you had made a mistake."

"I couldn't. I didn't."

"I ask you to use your imagination."

"I can't. Why are you going on like this? Why can't you let your poor mother rest in peace?"

"Because I want to know whether you are the same as those other women, because I don't want to make a fool of myself. I never go with women. But sometimes I meet one who reminds me of my mother. 'That is the one,' I tell myself."

"Does this happen often?"

"Not often, of course. Sometimes they are people I meet, but more often I think I see her in photographs. I used to buy all those magazines with pictures in them of weddings and house-parties. The people were not always identified. I have been sure I saw her face. I've made enquiries, written to people, gone to endless trouble. I have thousands of those magazines, Miss Kelly, literally thousands."

"But tell me, and please don't be offended—don't you think you may imagine it?"

"Imagine it?"

"Well, I mean, if the photos you showed me are like your mother, I don't think they are in the least like me. Do you? Really? Now, what's the matter? Are you all right, Mr Robinson?"

"I have this awful buzzing in my head. I've had it all day."

"Oh, my dear, why didn't you tell me? I have every kind of pain killer. Wait there and I'll bring you something for your poor head."

She came back soon with the contents of a medicine chest on a tray.

"Take two of these," she said, choosing the pills herself. "And wash them down with some of this." She had poured brandy into two glasses, larger ones by far than she was accustomed to.

She settled him on the sofa.

"Rest yourself there. Put your legs up." Nursing Mr Robinson was ever so much easier than dealing with him when he seemed well. She sat at the end of the sofa and held his hand. He closed his eyes and seemed to have fallen asleep. Miss Kelly leaned forward to inspect his face in repose. Her eyes were close to his when he opened them.

"Might I ask you for a little more of that good brandy?"

"By all means."

She helped herself at the same time. When the clock struck twelve, Miss Kelly said, very gently, "You had no sleep last night, and you have to be up early in the morning; don't you think you ought to go to bed?"

Mr Robinson muttered but made no attempt to move.

"I want to tell you before you go how immensely I admire you for what you did today."

"What did I do today?"

"Ringing Lynch up. It was the bravest thing a man ever did. I shall always respect you for it."

She slurred her speech a little. Mr Robinson's breath was redolent of brandy, but otherwise he showed no sign of the

187

evening's drinking. Going upstairs he walked with military precision. Miss Kelly held the banisters.

"Is your poor head better?" she enquired outside his door. "Let me see if Mrs Ridley gave you a hot-water bottle."

The bed was turned down. The bottle was there. Mr Robinson stood at the door like a sentry.

"Good night," Miss Kelly said and turned up her face.

"Good night," Mr Robinson said, and kissed it.

She lingered, but Mr Robinson still stood at attention.

"You are sure you have everything you want?" she said.

"Thank you."

"Good night," Miss Kelly said.

"Good night," said Mr Robinson.

In her room preparations had also been made; Mrs Ridley had laid out her nightdress on the bed. Miss Kelly undressed very quickly and was surprised to discover once her head lay on the pillow how wide awake she was. She heard a door open; she held her breath, her heart was beating fast; she heard (or did she hear?) footsteps in the corridor. Her door, in the gloom was hardly discernible, but she could, not having pulled the curtains, make out its outline against the lighter wallpaper. Did the handle turn, very slowly? Did the door slightly move? She thought so, and then she thought not. There was absolute silence in the house.

Out of doors, in the distance, some heavy lorry rumbled faintly. And, later, a dog barked in one of the farms across the fields. Then the clock in the hall wheezed, struck one, and wheezed again. That clock used to comfort Miss Kelly at night. It reminded her of Michael, making always the expected sound at the expected time, emphatically. There was a rustle as of a garment dragging along the ground; it stopped, then began again, then stopped. She sat up to locate the sound precisely and saw, against the window, the shadow of the branches of the climbing rose. She felt better sitting up. She turned on the light. That was the moment when Mr Robinson came into the room. He was wearing a white dressing-gown, tied very tightly round his waist with a cord.

She had heard the door opening; she knew it was he. She

188

spread her arms wide, but he looked for a chair and began to take off his dressing-gown. Miss Kelly buried her head in the pillow, but peeped out when minutes passed to see what was happening. Mr Robinson was then coming towards her. He was quite naked. It didn't seem to matter. She held up the bed-clothes to let him in. He would do whatever was to be done. She was ready. But Mr Robinson turned over at once and lay on his back. She waited. Then, moving closer, she whispered, "Shall I turn off the light?"

When he didn't answer, she did so and lay quite still. Very gently, she passed her hand over his face, taking an impression of each feature on her palm. He was nervous, she decided, and she let her hand move to the ring of hair on his hard chest. Timidly she kissed his ribs, little rabbit kisses.

Then Mr Robinson heaved himself up and brought his face close to hers.

"Put on the light," he said. He leaned on his elbow and looked at her, then pulled down the bedclothes. She was wear-ing a white sensible nightdress, one of six she bought in Harrods, some years before. Reaching up, she tried to put her hands around his neck.

"Shall I take it off?"

"No. No. . . . I like you as you are."

She began to sob. Very gently. She was rather drunk.

"Come," he said, excited now. "Sit beside me on the edge of the bed. Put your head on my shoulder. That's right. And that hand there."

She did as she was told. She was so pleased to let Mr Robinson take charge, she was prepared to fall in with any of his wishes, but to her way of thinking, it would have been far more comfort-able in bed. He began to talk very fast, and as he talked he pressed her closer and closer to him. She found it hard to breathe.

"Remember," he was saying, not whispering, talking very loud. "Remember when we sat like this?"

"I remember," she said.

"Your head on my shoulder. My arms around you?"

"I remember."

"And the sound of the sea?"

"I remember."

"And those people behind us? I thought they would never go."

"The Donnellys. You were disgracing me. I was very cross."

"They had their car lights on at first; but after a while they turned them off, and we sat in darkness. For hours."

"You are making this up."

"No. No. Your head was there, and my arm was there. And I could hear the sea. The sea never changes. It's out there waiting now. What would that couple have thought if they had known what we were up to! They turned off their car lights. Then they sat like this. Her head on his shoulder. His arm where mine is. For hours and hours. Then they drove away. Remember?"

"Only the Donnellys. There was no one else. And it was in broad daylight. That's why I was so cross."

"And we never moved, never said a word. Remember? And you wore that white nightdress. White. Pure white. It shone in the dark. Remember? And when I slipped you into the sea, it spread out on the water. Like a flower. Remember?"

Miss Kelly screamed "O-O-O-O". Very loud. And he knew she had remembered.

"Stop that," he said after a while. "Why can't you hold your noise?"

When Miss Kelly continued to scream he knew only one way of stopping her.

Whether Mr Robinson was to blame, or Miss Kelly if it came to that—and it did—you must decide for yourselves.

THE FIERCEST HEART

Stuart Cloete

Overcoming savage natives who oppose their advance,
surviving through fire, flood and disease, withstanding
treachery in their midst, the Boer Trekkers of the 1830s made
history.

THE FIERCEST HEART vividly tells the story of one such
group of Trekkers. Led by Willem Prinsloo they gather their
every possession and leave the security of their Cape Colony
home in search of a new Canaan far from British rule.

The enchanting Cina, Prinsloo's orphaned grand-daughter
travels with them. A beautiful questing child when they leave,
a woman — who has seen more than most do in a lifetime —
when they find their new home, she embodies the fiery
independence of the pioneer spirit.

A well-deserved classic of South African fiction THE FIERCEST
HEART is a powerful colourful and passionate tale of the
courage and determination of a displaced people in search
of a new land.

Futura Publications
Fiction
0 7088 2626 1

All Futura Books are available at your bookshop or
newsagent, or can be ordered from the following address:
Futura Books, Cash Sales Department,
P.O. Box 11, Falmouth, Cornwall.

Please send cheque or postal order (no currency), and
allow 55p for postage and packing for the first book plus
22p for the second book and 14p for each additional book
ordered up to a maximum charge of £1.75 in U.K.

Customers in Eire and B.F.P.O. please allow 55p for the
first book, 22p for the second book plus 14p per copy for
the next 7 books, thereafter 8p per book.

Overseas customers please allow £1 for postage and
packing for the first book and 25p per copy for each
additional book.